Sherlo

In the

Nautilus Adventure

By

Joseph W. Svec III

&

Lidia B. Svec

© Copyright 2016 Joseph W. Svec III

The right of Joseph W. Svec III to be identified as the author of this work has been asserted by him in accordance with the Copyright, Designs and Patents Act 1998.
All rights reserved. No reproduction, copy or transmission of this publication may be made without express prior written permission.
No paragraph of this publication may be reproduced, copied or transmitted except with express prior written permission or in accordance with the provisions of the Copyright Act 1956 (as amended). Any person who commits any unauthorized act in relation to this publication may be liable to criminal prosecution and civil claims for damage.
All characters appearing in this work are fictitious or used fictitiously. Except for certain historical personages, any resemblance to real persons, living or dead, is purely coincidental.
The opinions expressed herein are those of the authors and not of MX Publishing.
Paperback ISBN 978-1-78092-903-3
ePub ISBN 978-1-78092-904-0
PDF ISBN 978-1-78092-905-7

Published in the UK by MX Publishing 335 Princess Park Manor, Royal Drive, London, N11 3GX www.mxpublishing.co.uk
Cover design by www.staunch.com

Chapter header images licensed from Clipart. The author may be contacted via the web page, www.pixymuse.com
or via the Facebook page, www.facebook.com/sherlockgrinningcat

Acknowledgments:

I would like to acknowledge Linda Hein and Beth Barnard for their time and effort in editing this manuscript. It is greatly appreciated.

Thank you Harold and Jerold Lundgren for creating the outstanding handmade model of the Nautilus that is seen on the front cover.

I would like to acknowledge the encouragement of my son, Joe, and daughter, Leedjia Svec.

Dedication

This book is dedicated to my childhood sweetheart, best friend, soulmate, and bride of 43 years, Lidia. You are talented and gifted. You are my inspiration and my Pixy Muse. Thank you for co-authoring this book with me.

Sherlock Holmes in the Nautilus Adventure

Table of Contents:

A Note to Readers:

Prologue: A Memorandum from Dr. Watson

Chapter 1. A Most Unusual Visitor, (But not to be unexpected after the day's previous events.)

Chapter 2. A Most Unusual Tale, (And certainly a bit fishy.)

Chapter 3. A Most Unusual Journey, (And a good deal of seafood along the way.)

Chapter 4. A Most Unusual Clue, (And a very helpful dolphin.)

Chapter 5. A Most Unusual Discovery, (And who would have ever imagined it?)

Chapter 6. A Most Unusual Lead, (But certainly rather timely.)

Chapter 7. A Most Unusual Sight, (So there is some truth to that old tale.)

Chapter 8. A Most Unusual Turn of Events, (But Sherlock saw it coming.)

Chapter 9. One More Most Unusual Turn of Events, (Who would have imagined yet another lost civilization?

Chapter 10. A Most Unusual Dilemma, (And a new plan of action.)

Chapter 11. Another Most Unusual Journey, (And a very quick one at that.)

Chapter 12. A Most Unusual Plan, (As well as a good deal of ice.)

Chapter 13. A Most Unusual Sequence of Events, (And a glowing success.)

Chapter 14. A Most Unusual Volcanic Eruption, (And a pleasant reunion.)

Chapter 15. Yet, Another Most Unusual Journey, (And Sherlock plays the violin!)

Chapter 16. Yet, Another Most Unusual Discovery, (And I am certain that Sherlock suspects something.)

Chapter 17. A Most Unusual Revelation, (And who would question it considering the source?)

Chapter 18. A Most Unusual Way to Stop an Auxiliary Steam Ship, (But it went quite well, all things considered.)

Chapter 19. A Most Unusual Solution, (And it's amazing what a good cup of tea can do.)

Chapter 20. A Most Unusual Situation, (And some excellent wine.)

Chapter 21. Another Most Unusual Plan, (And I think Sherlock is still being vague.)

Chapter 22. A Most Unusual Confrontation, (And it turns out a good cup of tea is the answer.)

Chapter 23. A Most Unusual Conclusion, (And a sad farewell, but an encouraging promise.)

Post script: Again? (Yes, it can get even more strange and unusual.)

A Note to Readers:

The following manuscript, Sherlock Holmes in the Nautilus Adventure, is part of a recently rediscovered collection of papers belonging to a Dr. John Watson, M.D. He was a noted surgeon and the biographer of Sherlock Holmes, a famous consulting detective who lived in Victorian England. Sherlock Holmes is the best known detective in history, having solved the most baffling cases that confounded Scotland Yard. His skills in observation, perception, deduction and logic are beyond compare. His career was founded on seeing what no one else did, and understanding its overall significance in the matters at hand. Dr. Watson recorded and published many of Holmes' more fascinating cases and adventures.

This particular tale, along with several other manuscripts found at the same time, had been requested by Dr. Watson to be set aside and not published for varying periods of time due to the unusual nature of the subject matter. I concur with him in that the content is indeed very unusual and at times difficult to accept. Sometime during the waiting period, the manuscripts were misplaced and forgotten until their recent discovery. As the requested waiting period has long since passed, they may be published without concern; however the reader may be quite surprised by certain aspects of the stories due to the unique nature of these adventures, which are far different from the typical solving of a murder or locating a missing object. Be advised. In reading Sherlock Holmes in the Nautilus Adventure, you are in for a most unusual voyage literally and figuratively. Let it be said, "The game's afloat!"

Prologue

Memorandum:

To: Whom it may Concern
From: Dr. John Watson M.D.
Subject: *Sherlock Holmes in the Nautilus Adventure*
Date: February, 1898

Everyone knows that Captain Nemo is the fictional main character of Jules Verne's novel, *Twenty Thousand Leagues Under the Sea*. That was my belief as well before we began the amazing journey that I recount in this manuscript. The reader will discover, as I did, there is much more to Captain Nemo than Jules Verne revealed. As I recall the adventure that unfolded, it is with great awe, and a certain sense of sorrow with which I write this. I find myself once again in admiration of Sherlock Holmes's abilities in logic and deduction and how he saved the world from a threat that few people alive today are aware of. But it is also with sadness that I remember a fond farewell that is still heavy in my heart.

While every word of this is true, it is too fantastic and unusual to be published during my life time. For the sake of my reputation as a doctor, the confidence of my patients, and the name of Sherlock Holmes, I ask that this manuscript not be published until seventy five years after my passing. Your compliance in this request is greatly appreciated.

Dr. John H. Watson M.D.

Sherlock Holmes in the Nautilus Adventure

Chapter 1. A Most Unusual Visitor,
(But not to be unexpected after the day's previous events.)

I looked at the gentleman standing there before us in Sherlock's parlor with utter disbelief. "You can't be serious!" I exclaimed. "Are you saying that YOU are Captain Nemo, the main character from Jules Verne's novel, *"Twenty Thousand Leagues under the Sea?"* Everyone knows that story is a fictional adventure novel. The next thing you will be saying is that you have the *Nautilus* docked right outside the front door of 221-B Baker Street!"

"Actually it is currently submerged in London Harbor, waiting for a signal from me to surface and pick us up," he replied rather straightforwardly.

"Us?" Sherlock responded, raising one eyebrow with a quizzical look. "And who exactly is us?"

This was too much already! Sherlock Holmes and I no sooner had resolved The Adventure of the Grinning Cat, which I thought without question was certainly the strangest adventure of his career, and now this! As you recall, in the Grinning Cat adventure, the Cheshire Cat, White Rabbit, and Hatter from Lewis Carroll's *"Alice in Wonderland"*, had appeared at 221-B Baker Street seeking Sherlock's help in locating Alice who had disappeared from Wonderland, as well as Lewis Carroll himself whom they also could not locate. This visit resulted in us taking several aerial trips over London, visiting Alice's Wonderland, and eventually stepping outside of time itself. Between time travels into other realities, fictional characters coming to life, and meeting a Unicorn, as well as a dragon of sorts, it was one very illogical, strange, and curious adventure.

Now we had yet another visitor claiming to be a well known fictional character, who was looking for his author who had gone missing. As unusual as it all seemed, I must say that the gentleman standing before us certainly did look the part of the person he was claiming to be. He was tall and well built, had a neatly trimmed dark beard, and a certain bearing about him that portrayed confidence, leadership, and an air of ageless wisdom. His eyes were wide set giving him a broad range of vision and were of the deepest blue that I had ever seen. I could not determine his nationality. His dark blue uniform was well used but meticulous, and his jacket bore the letter "N" in gold thread upon the breast pocket surrounded by the circular phrase,

"Mobili e Mobilus". Now if you have read Jules Verne's novel, then you are aware that that the "N" stands for his vessel the *Nautilus*, while the phrase surrounding it is Latin for "Moving in the moving element." Yes, this stranger really did look like the fictional Captain Nemo brought to life. But how was it possible?

I turned to Holmes and asked, "What is your opinion on this, Sherlock? Have all boundaries between reality and literary fiction completely collapsed? What do you think is going on here? Do you believe this really is Captain Nemo of the *Nautilus*? How on earth would that be feasible?"

The tall stern-faced gentleman turned to me with a deep penetrating look and replied, "I understand your skepticism, Dr. Watson. You are a doctor, not a scientist." Then with a slow wave of his hand, as if pointing out the night sky, he stated, "This must seem as inconceivable as perhaps a trek through the stars. You do not know the full story behind Jules Verne's novel. Perhaps it would help if I explained. May I sit down?"

"Yes indeed," Sherlock responded, gesturing towards a chair. "May we offer you some tea?"

"No thank you, just some hot water." Captain Nemo replied, holding up a small tea tin. "I prefer my own seaweed based blend. It's quite excellent you know, very healthy and beneficial for one's constitution. I drink it every day. You are welcome to try it, and I think it would be quite good for you as well as enjoyable." Looking at us both he asked, "Would you care for some?"

13

As a part of my medical practice, I had heard of the exceptional medicinal qualities of certain seaweeds, but somehow I could not fathom a tea made from seaweed being enjoyable. Still, I did not think it would hurt, and Sherlock had quickly agreed, so Holmes indulged our guest, and he poured three cups of hot water into which Captain Nemo added his seaweed tea blend. The aroma was quite different and seemed to fill the room with a salt sea air that set the mood for the unusual tale that I thought was sure to follow. Little did I know where it was to lead.

We sipped our seaweed tea as Captain Nemo began to speak. His words issued forth as if an ocean fog had permeated the room; Nemo's voice being a distant fog horn, fading in and out. It was there and then gone, somewhere out in the distance. Even the room seemed as if it was moving, or perhaps "floating" would be the better word. I felt myself drifting away and losing consciousness. I tried to resist, but the pull of the tide was too strong. Darkness was enveloping me like a sea mist. In the strange twilight, it felt like tentacles of an octopus were grabbing hold of me and carrying me somewhere while odd voices whispered in the background. I heard the chime of a ship's bell tolling somewhere nearby. Then, all was silent.

The next thing I remember was waking up in a rather comfortable, velvet upholstered chair in a compact, but well-appointed room that was certainly not 221-B Baker Street. While the finish work of the salon was of the highest quality with red velvet furniture, varnished mahogany panels, polished brass, crystals and fine materials, the ceiling looked like it was made entirely of metal with pipes and gauges in place. The floors were covered with elegant Persian rugs. The walls contained fabulous works of art as well as shelves full of books and marine life specimens, and there was a large pipe organ against the far wall. Somewhere in the background, I could hear the rhythmic pulsing of some type of machinery, and there was coolness to the air. With rising fear and trepidation, I realized that somehow, as strange as it seemed, I was actually aboard Captain Nemo's submersible vessel the *Nautilus*.

Panicking, I glanced about and saw Holmes calmly sitting in a plush chair across from me holding a cup of tea and talking with our strange guest. "Sherlock!" I cried out, "The tea! It was drugged!"

Holmes raised the tea cup in his hand as if to salute me and calmly replied, "Yes, yes, Watson. I know it was. You don't expect something that simple to escape my astute perception and knowledge of all things related to narcotics, do you? I knew what it was as soon as he added it to the hot water. Don't you remember? Last year I wrote a monograph on *"The Therapeutic, Narcotic and Hallucinogenic Characteristics and Effects of Various Seaweeds of the Atlantic Ocean"*. As a result of my previous experimentations and test samples with seaweed (all in the name of forensic science, you know), the tea had no effect on me whatsoever."

He paused to make a wide sweep of his hand, to emphasize our surroundings and pointed out. "I am sure you can tell that we are indeed on board Captain Nemo's *Nautilus*. It's really quite remarkable. In fact, it is far more so than Verne's novel even began to indicate. Jules Verne is an excellent writer, but this! This vessel is beyond the power of description. It's too bad you were not awake. I had to help him carry you aboard myself. Did you know you were mumbling something about an octopus? Captain Nemo provided enough information after you passed out for me to determine that we really must assist him in this matter. He was just going into more details, when you came to. Perhaps he won't mind repeating a few of the finer points for you."

My mind was still foggy from the after effects of the tea, but if Sherlock said it was alright to trust this odd stranger, then I knew that I should, but still...

Captain Nemo stood up, and held out his hand to me as he began speaking. "First I must apologize for the ruse with the tea. I could not be certain you would believe me when I told you my story, and the stakes are simply too high to fail. I thought that if I could just get you aboard the *Nautilus*, then you would see for yourselves and understand that it is all genuine. I truly am Captain Nemo of the *Nautilus*, and I must find Jules Verne. Sherlock Holmes is the only one in the world with the skills required to succeed in this task. So please do accept my apology, and indulge yourself in some refreshments. I assure you these are perfectly safe, and quite delectable."

I cautiously shook Nemo's hand in acceptance of the apology, looked at the table, which appeared to offer a wide variety of the ocean's bounty, and then at Sherlock. Holmes responded by nodding his head and expounding. "Don't be afraid of the seafood, Watson. It is all quite good. And the fried squid is particularly excellent."

Nemo then added. "The squid is my own special recipe and I get a certain sense of satisfaction each time I serve it. You do understand of course, that the encounter with the giant squid in the novel was based on fact."

My head was still swimming, and it felt as if the rest of me had not yet caught up. I thought that perhaps a bite or two might help, and the aroma was exotic as well as appetizing, so, I did help myself to the seafood offerings as Captain Nemo began his unusual tale.

Chapter 2. A Most Unusual Tale, (And certainly a bit fishy.)

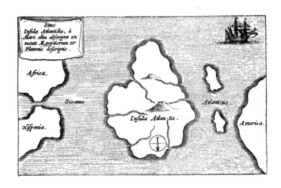

"Gentlemen, first of all, I want to say that what I am going to share with you is the truth. It may not agree with what you do or do not know about the world, history as it is taught, Jules Verne, his works, or for that matter, the representation of myself as a character in his novel, but it is true, every word of it.

There is a force, or should I say an organization, that exists behind the scenes and is invisible to the outside world. They have eyes almost everywhere... and more ears than eyes."

Hearing that, my own eyes grew wide with anticipation, and I inhaled deeply to express my concern, and almost as if he could read my mind, he continued.

"Don't be alarmed, Dr. Watson. They do not seek global domination or unlimited power. They have been monitoring this world since ancient times, observing its development and growth, giving it a nudge here or there as needed, or placing barriers when and where it is necessary. They are the Guardians of the world so to speak."

Recalling our dealings with the Guardians of Time in our last adventure earlier that day, I had to ask, "Are they any relation to the Time Guardians? I am sure your mysterious organization is aware of them if they are as all knowing as you say, and I cannot say that I am very fond of the Time Guardians' activities."

Nemo looked at me with clear, piercing eyes and continued. "Yes, Dr. Watson, the two are, in fact, somewhat related. The Time Guardians are actually special entities, if I may call them that, whose task it is to keep time functioning in an orderly manner. They are extremely powerful in many ways. If there are too many random time travelers, things could get quite sticky, and you might end up with someone driving a Delorian automobile into the past and then back to the future and really messing things up."

Holmes raised his eyebrow and interjected. "But since we have not seen any 'Delorians' whatever they may happen to be, I deduct that things related to time are currently functioning properly and in a timely manner, so to speak."

Nemo nodded and agreed. "Yes, related to time, things are generally as they should be. The time wanderings of Lewis Carroll and H. G. Wells, or those of Jules Verne, have not adversely affected the order of things. On the contrary, they have helped keep things on track. As I said earlier, sometimes humanity needs a little nudge, and authors like H. G. Wells and Mr. Verne have provided it in a subtle yet effective manner."

Holmes leaned forward and asked. "Are you telling me that their works of fictional science or 'science fiction,' if I may call it that, are actually planting the seeds for the inventions and scientific achievements of the future?"

Captain Nemo smiled and relaxed a bit. "Yes, that's it precisely. By reading fictional accounts about the wondrous achievements and the terrifying horrors of the future, humanity can be gently guided in the right direction and eventually take its proper place in the grand scheme of things. That is why we are here, to ensure that it does happen at the right time. But there are those individuals and governments that would misuse the knowledge and the power that comes with such information, to gain control over the world. We also must be cautious and watchful to prevent that from happening."

"So you are saying that you are one of this organization of guardians?" Holmes asked slowly.

Captain Nemo paused a moment, looked squarely at Sherlock, and replied, "Yes, I am. From my vessel the *Nautilus*, I have been observing humanity and its use of the ocean for centuries. I can tell you that more than one sea monster over the ages has been attributed to this ship. Cetus, Kraken, Devil Whale, Leviathan, Iku-Turso, the list is endless. All of them refer to the *Nautilus*. On many different occasions we have even been identified as a Giant Narwhale.

He paused and looked at Holmes and then me and went on. "Jules Verne's novel is a fictional version of my adventures with enough modifications that our real organization and its purpose remained a secret."

"So is he a member of your group also?" I interjected.

"No, no! Not at all," The Captain replied. "Verne, Wells, and Carroll are all human enough, but they are also quite gifted so that they were able to see through the veil and learn how to travel in time and benefit from it, while we were able to use their fictional accounts and novels to our advantage."

Pointing directly at Holmes, he elaborated. "Mr. Holmes, now that you have broken through the veil and discovered time travel, you too will have an outstanding advantage in your line of work. Your powers of perception and deduction, which up to now have been rather good, in the future will seem absolutely uncanny. Your deductions and conclusions will seem next to impossible to the average intellect."

Then looking at me he added, "And you too have an impressive task in front of you, Dr. Watson. Not one word of this can be included in your chronologies of Mr. Holmes' adventures and cases. There must be no mention whatsoever of time travel anywhere in the adventures of Sherlock Holmes during your time period. Yes, you can record this adventure and the real truth, but it must remain unpublished for at least 75 years. By then it may be safe let the truth be known. Or it may have to wait longer. Only time will tell for sure."

Captain Nemo paused, took a sip of his tea, and after a waiting a moment for the impact of his story to sink in, he looked in Sherlock's direction and went on. "You really did do a remarkable job of resolving the Wonderland and Lewis Carroll problem. When you solved that final logic puzzle so quickly, we knew that you would be the one we could turn to regarding our current problem, but only if you could accept the reality of it all. As I stated earlier, that is why I had to get you both on board the *Nautilus*, so you can comprehend the truth of it all."

Holmes nodded his head in agreement and replied, "We understand that you and the *Nautilus* do exist, and you have related a fascinating story, but what is the nature of the Jules Verne problem at hand? And what per chance did you mean by "Verne, Wells and Carroll are human enough"? Are you saying that you are not human? And if you are not human, if you don't mind me asking, what exactly are you? I also note you allude to the fact you are centuries old. If that is the case, I must say you look rather well for your age. I shall have to rewrite my essay on *"Calculating a Person's Age Accurately to Within one Month Based on Readily Observable but Generally Overlooked Attributes and Characteristics."*

Captain Nemo set his tea cup down, sighed, clasped his hands together in front of himself, and stared at a point somewhere in the distance, as if he were trying to figure out where to begin answering Holmes' questions. The silence was heavy with anticipation, as we waited for his reply, while in the background the humming of some sort of machinery could faintly be heard. I again looked around the luxurious salon in which we sat, dumfounded that all of this was in a submersible vessel traveling underwater.

Captain Nemo finally broke the silence and continued. "So many questions. So very many questions... Yes, you need answers to all of them to fully grasp the situation. What exactly am I? You have heard of 'Atlantis the Lost Continent', I am sure. In fact, Jules Verne even mentioned it in his novel. But the sunken ruins he spoke of are just the surface of the story. Eons ago, the Earth was populated by a people that were put here by the Creator. Things went well enough for quite some time. Atlantis was truly magnificent beyond description. It was a wellspring of creativity, art, music, science, medicine, and knowledge such as humanity has never known. But perhaps their knowledge was too great, their thirst for more too demanding. Despite the objections from those of us that saw the danger, the leaders eventually lost their way and destroyed it all in a great cataclysm that sank Atlantis beneath the waves forever. But some of us escaped the destruction. In fact, it was the *Nautilus* that made it possible. Yes, the *Nautilus* was the pride of the Atlantean Navy. At one time, she was a research vessel. Now she is all that is left of our civilization.

"Eventually, humanity as you know it now was given its second chance on Earth. That's the current lot of you, by the way. We survivors of Atlantis vowed to watch over you and never let what happened to us happen to you as well. The Creator agreed and decided to let us remain here nearly invisible, behind the scenes, watching and guiding humanity until we can be certain they are not going to repeat our mistake.

In order to do that, we were given greatly extended life spans. We have become the organization of watchers and guardians that I mentioned at the beginning of my story, subtly placed in key areas around the world monitoring and guiding your development.

"I know humanity has experienced its darker periods. The atrocities have at times been terrible over the centuries. But there has always been a light in the darkness, and you have pulled yourselves out of it. At times, it was with our help and at times you have done it on your own. We are proud of how far you have come."

Nemo hesitated a moment, took a deep breath, and exhaled. "We have been quite secretive about our presence, only accepting into our confidence those individuals such as yourselves and Mr. Verne, whom we were absolutely certain we could trust. However, someone or some group knows about us. Who it is or how much they know is uncertain, but they are the ones who have kidnapped Jules Verne. This much we do know."

Holmes interrupted the tale and asked, "How long has Mr. Verne been missing? Has his absence been noticed yet?"

"He has only been gone one day, and his absence has not yet been noticed, as he is supposedly off on a trip in his former auxiliary steam yacht the *Saint-Michel III*. He sold it several years ago, but just recently he received an unexpected invitation from the current owner to take a short cruise. The vessel happened to be in the area where Jules Verne was at the time, and it was to be a short cruise, "for old times' sake," as the new owner put it. Verne naturally accepted. We found the vessel adrift and abandoned in the middle of the English Channel. We now have some of my crew on board continuing the course that had been planned out in the log book, so nothing looks suspicious. There were signs of a struggle, and we found this. We have never seen anything like it before."

He held up a strange object that appeared to be a round metal disc or a medallion with a miniature star map, compass rose, and the stylized letter "M" superimposed upon it.

"As much as we have eyes everywhere and are masters at observing your world, we are not omnipotent, and sadly, we do not have all of the answers. That is why we need someone with your observational skills and deductive abilities, Mr. Holmes. We need you to locate Jules Verne before anything worse happens to him. His captors are most likely planning to gain from him his method of time travel and whatever scientific knowledge of the future he has. That would be a catastrophe. Can we count on your support, Mr. Holmes? I know you most recently have saved Wonderland, but now the fate of your entire world depends on you."

Chapter 3. A Most Unusual Journey, (And a great deal of seafood on the way.)

Sherlock examined the object carefully, looked at the back side of it, turned it over again, and commented, "I should like to examine Mr. Verne's sailing yacht for additional clues as soon as possible. If this object came from whom I think it did, Mr. Verne is in grave danger, and we must act quickly. But if your organization has access to the river of time and time travel as you allude to, why can you not just go back to the moment that he was abducted and intervene?"

Captain Nemo shook his head and replied. "An excellent question, Mr. Holmes, but over the course of the centuries, all of us Atlanteans remaining have reached the limits of our ability to time travel and no longer have access to that path. Yes, the Time Guardians are a part of our legacy, but they too must obey the rules that have been set forth. With Lewis Carroll deceased, H. G. Wells having reached his limit and being no longer able to time travel, and Jules Verne being kidnapped, the only potential time traveler left is you.

"But I must warn you: As astute in logic as you are, you too must play by "The Rules," so to speak. Your opportunities to time travel are not unlimited, and I caution you to use them wisely so you will have that availability when you need it the most. You know your own skills, Mr. Holmes, and only you can determine when to play that card. And it will be a very tricky card to play, considering the method that you used to step outside of the River of Time. I believe it involved a Unicorn, a Dragon, and several other literary characters. I know enough of your reputation to trust your judgment in that matter. If you'll excuse me for just a moment, I will have a course set to intercept the *Saint-Michel III*."

Captain Nemo turned a switch on a small control panel on a nearby pedestal and spoke into a device on the end of curved tube. He addressed his crew on the other end of the device, in a language unintelligible to me, and all at once in the background, there were sounds of the propulsion system increasing in power. I could feel a boost in speed. There was additional conversation between Nemo and his crew, and then he shut off the switch and turned to us.

"We will intercept the *Saint-Michel III* in less than a day. You seem to have an idea as to who might be behind this. Might I ask his name?"

Sherlock thought in silence for a moment and replied, "The initial "M" and graphics on the object lead me to believe it could possibly be a Professor James Moriority, but I will not say for certain until I see more evidence. He is a mathematical and astronomical genius and a mastermind of criminal activity and other evil doings, yet he has managed to keep his name spotlessly clean. The last I heard, he was controlling all of London's criminal activities from behind the scenes, but this sounds like something much farther than his reach. With all of the contacts he has, he could have found out about your presence, but the question is, how much does the kidnapper of Jules Verne know? Tell me about your network of Atlanteans. How many of you exist? Where are you posted? How do you communicate between yourselves? It is obvious there has been a compromise in your communication channels. We must find out where."

Captain Nemo nodded his head in concurrence and replied, "Well, we have one in the senior staff of the American President, Benjamin Harrison, and another is the in staff of the British Prime Minister, Robert Cecil. We have agents within and closely monitoring the governments of France, Germany, Poland, Russia, China, and Japan. We have twelve others positioned in the academic and scientific communities around the world, keeping an eye on developments. And there is myself and my crew. My crew members and I rarely leave the *Nautilus*, so I doubt it could have been any one of us. We believe that our Atlantean language is incomprehensible to humans, so we communicate relatively freely via post or telegraph and also using our wireless long distance communication devices."

Sherlock replied. "You mentioned you and your Atlantean companions have unnaturally long lives. How do your people prevent that from being noticed?"

"The crew of the *Nautilus* and I have no need to. As I mentioned, we are a rather closed group. Those Atlanteans who are outside of my crew quietly disappear and then reappear in a different country with a new identity and sometimes minor changes in appearance. A change of hair color or the addition or deletion of facial hair does wonders, as you would know. You are quite the master of disguise, as I understand. It is unlikely that any of them would be noticed."

Sherlock nodded as he answered, "Yes, I could see that. Returning to your Atlantean language that you believe is incomprehensible to us; may I see a written sample of it? Is it possible that your group has been too lax and someone has deciphered and translated it? Last year, I wrote a paper on, *"Using Logic Based Perception and Mathematical Based Rational to Translate Ciphers, Codes and Unintelligible Languages with a Focus on Mythical Greek Writings"*. Now that I think of it, I did get a letter from someone identifying himself as a language scholar asking for clarification on an issue. I dismissed it at the time, but there may be a connection."

"I will see to it that you get some samples of Atlantean communications, Mr. Holmes. Right now I have to attend to some ship's business. If you will excuse me, I should be back in a moment."

Captain Nemo again spoke in to the communication device, and then stepped out of the room.

"Well Holmes," I asked, "What do you think of all this? Honestly, this sound's more farfetched than a talking cat telling us that Alice is missing from Wonderland and a Unicorn telling us that the H. G. Wells has the answer. And you know how that all turned out. It got stranger still."

"Yes, Watson, it is quite unusual. I will grant you that. But there is logic to it if you can accept the facts that are given. We are, in fact, on board the *Nautilus* traveling far beneath the ocean's surface." And with that he pushed a lever in front of a circular metal iris, which then spun open to reveal a very large porthole. It was big enough to be called a window actually, and it showed us the expanse of the ocean floor as we journeyed on our way to intercept Jules Verne's former yacht. It was astonishing and hypnotizing to see the depths of sea unfold before us. A rainbow of marine life was displayed before my eyes. I saw several schools of multicolored fish arrayed in a wide assortment of different shades and hues. There were green sea turtles, grey and white sharks, and more. Off in the distance the aquamarine filament faded away into an inky azure darkness that concealed countless mysteries I was captivated until Sherlock pulled the lever and closed the iris.

"Tell me Watson, how can we be seeing all that if we are not on board the *Nautilus*?" It is the only logical conclusion. I believe what Captain Nemo says is true, and I also suspect that their language code has been broken. In fact, I may have inadvertently helped someone do it. That is all the more reason why I need to help them solve this disappearance."

At that moment, a crew member holding several letters written in Atlantean, entered the salon and handed them to Sherlock. "These are for you, Mr. Holmes. The Captain said if you need more samples to just ask, and I will get them for you." The crew member turned and left the salon and as he did, the door closed with a metallic echo that emphasized the unique strangeness of our surroundings.

Holmes was instantly lost in his examination and study of the Atlantean language. I was left to my own accord for some time. I wandered around the salon enjoying the bountiful selection of seafood that was available on the table, and I must say the sautéed squid was particularly excellent. I also examined the specimens of marine life and other items on display. In addition to the corals and sea shells, there were many priceless works of art. There were also volumes of literary works and scientific papers on the shelves. I even spotted one of Sherlock's works, *"An Analysis of Tea Consumption in Relation to One's Likelihood of Attending Violin Concerts"*. As I recall, that paper provided critical information in solving a significant mystery in the upper levels of London society.

We were quite a distance from London society now, however. Considering the previous day's adventure and where it had led us, I wondered where on earth we would end up next, if indeed it was still on earth. The way things were going we could end up in the belly of a whale or something even more unbelievable. That is not to say where we were at that moment was not truly astounding. The background hum of the machinery continued, and I again opened the iris to watch for quite some time in fascination as the *Nautilus* propelled its way through the never ending mysteries of the undersea world.

Holmes was oblivious to me while he worked on deciphering the Atlantean language. He said nothing other than to request more tea, which was only an arm's length away from him, but that is Sherlock when he is immersed in resolving a problem. He also asked me to procure one additional Atlantean letter. I closed the metal iris and poured him another cup of tea. Since I did not know how their communication device worked, I had to knock on the door of the salon to get a crew member's attention to obtain one more sample letter. The metallic echo reverberated through our surroundings. With Sherlock having recently solved a nearly impossible logic puzzle, I imagined that this must have been much simpler for him, but he continued to work on it in silence, shuffling the letters back and forth and madly writing out lines of text on the note pad.

After some time had passed, Captain Nemo returned to let us know that we would be approaching Jules Verne's former yacht very soon and that as a precaution; he had started using a code in addition to their language. Holmes responded by handing

Nemo complete translations of the sample letters and saying. "I understand your concern in wanting to use a code. I have just finished translating your Atlantean language. If I have done so that means someone else could have done so as well, even if they are not as talented as I. However, if we know someone is eavesdropping, we could use that in our favor and feed them misinformation. We could possibly even set up a trap."

Nemo stared at the translations and muttered, "So that is how it was done. All these years we believed our language was a safe communication method. Yes, I see your point. We wouldn't want to let on that we know that they know, whoever "they" may be. That is excellent logic, Mr. Holmes, but we don't know specifically where the messages are being intercepted."

"Understood," agreed Holmes, "which is why I suggest that we send our doctored message out to one Atlantean recipient at a time and watch for the result that tells us it has been read by someone outside of your group. It will be simple for me to come up with a message that will get their attention and cause them to react in a way that will be obvious to us. Just leave that to me."

Captain Nemo smiled and stated firmly, "Excellent, Mr. Holmes. I am pleased that we can count on you, but first your observational and deductive skills are needed topside. I can tell by our reduced speed that we are alongside the *Saint-Michel III*. We will be surfacing momentarily."

Chapter 4. A Most Unusual Clue, (And a very helpful dolphin.)

I had hardly noticed it, but the ship's speed had decreased while Captain Nemo was speaking. He indicated to us to follow him out of the salon and up a spiral metal staircase that led to a bridge/control room area that had two bulbous round view ports on the forward bulkheads. I could see that we had already surfaced while we were on our way to the bridge. There were several crew members present, with one of them at the wheel, while the remainders were positioned at various stations and other controls. What any of the controls might have been used for, I had no idea. I had never seen anything like it before.

A crew member spoke in English as we entered. "The *Nautilus* is matching her speed sir, and we have rigged a boarding plank and guy lines to get across to her."

Nemo nodded towards us as he left the bridge and stated, "Gentlemen, if you will follow me."

We followed Captain Nemo as he exited through an open doorway in the aft bulkhead of the control room. It felt good to be topside in the open air again. The brisk sea wind had a crisp, salty tang to it, and the sea spray felt good after being below. Looking forward, I could see the arched ramming spur of Captain Nemo's vessel. His submersible reminded me of a large metal shark slicing through the swells. She was the perfect coalescence of nature and technology. Cruising very close to the *Nautilus* was a beautiful white- hulled, auxiliary steam yacht of approximately one hundred feet in length. She was clipper bowed and schooner rigged with raked masts. Her lines were sleek, and she was moving along smartly. As I gazed at her bounding through the waves, she whispered softly of the romance and mystery of the sea. A plank had been run between them with guy lines stretched waist high on either side.

The Captain pointed to the yacht and stated, "That is Jules Verne's former yacht, the *Saint-Michel III*. She is quite beautiful, but we are not here to admire her lines. I am hoping you can find some additional clues that we may have overlooked, Mr. Holmes."

Holmes immediately replied, "I can see a vessel of this size would require a crew of at least ten, and you had mentioned there was the new owner that had invited him. Do you have any idea what happened to them at the time Jules Verne disappeared?"

"That's the strange part. The crew and new owner disappeared with Verne, but the ship's lifeboats are not missing. As I mentioned, there were some small signs of a struggle, some things knocked over on deck and in the cabin that appears to have been used by Jules Verne, but there was no trace of bloodshed. Our replacement crew was instructed to leave everything as it was found, as much as possible, when we discovered her. We had hoped that we could convince you to help us figure out just what had happened here and did not want to disturb any evidence beyond that odd token that I showed you earlier."

Holmes was already on the gangplank, walking between the two vessels as he called back, "A wise choice, Captain Nemo. I will investigate and let you know what I find. I am certain there may be clues on board that are invisible to the untrained eye."

Holmes quickly traveled the distance and was on board when he called out to me, "You come too, Watson. Your assistance is required here."

I looked at the narrow walkway that was strung between the two moving vessels in the rolling seas and was about to object when I recalled some of the journeys that I had taken earlier during the Grinning Cat adventure. Surely this could not be as bad as being inside a carriage being flown all over London by a Jabberwocky trying to follow a Unicorn at top speed. And those Time Machine journeys were something I would never want to experience again. With a firm resolve, I stepped onto the plank only to notice several fins in the water between the two vessels.

My first thought was: Sharks! Needless to say, I nearly ran across the plank and made it to the other vessel even quicker than Sherlock.

As I stepped onto the deck of the *Saint-Michel III*, Holmes pointed at them and observed, "Look Watson! Those are common Atlantic Dolphins. *Delphinus Delphus* is the scientific name. Did you ever think you would see them so close in the wild? Rather exhilarating, isn't it?"

I looked back at them just in time to see one of them leap into the air and fall sideways back into the water with a large splash, completely soaking me with salt water. I was   about to remark on the less than enjoyable "exhilarating" dolphin when Holmes commented, "We have no time to play with the dolphins, Watson. Start scrutinizing to see if you can find anything that seems out of place. You have been with me on enough investigations to know what I am looking for. It is the common place yet nearly invisible trifle, which will reveal what, has happened here."

Still dripping with salt water, I began to walk around the deck to get a good look at things. Having spent very little time at sea, I was not certain what in fact I was looking for on board a steam yacht that would be unseen to the common eye. The Atlantean crew welcomed us on board and reiterated that they had not touched anything other than what was required to run the vessel. I was certain that I could see them smirking as I left a trail of "playful dolphin" seawater behind me. Everything looked normal enough. The masts, the rigging, the steam funnel, and other ship's gear were as one would expect. The creak of the rigging and the hull all seemed natural. How was I supposed to see the invisible?

Of course, Sherlock came out of the cabin that had been Verne's almost immediately waving a sheet of paper in his hand saying, "Take a look at this, Watson. What do you make of it? I found it in Verne's cabin. It was on the desk but quite cleverly hidden under the desk pad. It was essentially invisible. It looks like the start of a poem, but I am quite certain there is more to it. Verne was very adept at ciphers and hidden messages."

He handed me a sheet on which had been written in French the start of a poem that translated, read as follows:

"Salt Water

Salt water, salt water, the life blood of Earth.

Salt water, salt water, the source of our birth.

The answer you seek which is hidden from view,

is in the salt water that's all around you.

Fear not the creature that lives in the brine.

The life that she saves, it may be thine.

Salt water, salt water, the wide ocean blue

reveals the secret that's hidden from view."

As I held the paper, some of the salt water that was still dripping from my clothes ran across the paper and revealed additional writing that had been invisible just a moment before.

"Look at this Holmes!" I exclaimed. "The salt water is revealing a hidden message. You are right. There is more to this than just the start of a poem."

Holmes took the poem back, laid it flat on a cabin top, and asked me to wring my jacket sleeve over it, adding, "Good work, Watson. You should give your dolphin friend a treat for assisting us with this message."

I glanced back over the side, and the two dolphins were still keeping pace with the vessels. The nearer dolphin that had doused me did a spectacular leap that cleared the gangplank and guy lines before diving back into the water. As it leaped out of the water I noticed a white crescent shaped mark on the front of its head. I did ask one of the crew if there were any salted fish in the galley to give to the creature since it been so helpful. He laughed and went to see if he could find anything.

As the salt water moistened the remainder of the paper, additional writing came into view. Sherlock translated and read it aloud it as it appeared. *"I am in danger. The invitation to come on this cruise was a sham. The captain and crew are answering to somebody higher in command, and they intend on kidnapping me for reasons unbeknownst at this time. This vessel will be met by another shortly so I have little time. I overheard a conversation that indicated their base is less than 75 nautical miles from this position. Latitude N. 50,111'2", Longitude W.*

0,39'38". They appear to have great resources, so use caution. My life is in your hands, but Luna may be helpful. Trust her. Jules Verne."

We both stood in silence for just a moment before Sherlock requested a nautical chart of the area adding, "We have to determine where they are headed. With the speed of the *Nautilus*, we should be able to intercept them rather swiftly, but we need to know where they are."

Taking the chart from a crew member who had hurriedly brought it to him from the cabin, Sherlock spread it out on the cabin top and looking at the coordinates given in the letter stated, "This can't be right." Then using a belaying pin as a straight distance measure from the scale on the chart, he drew a circle with a radius of 75 nautical miles around the point given by Verne. There was no land whatsoever within the circumference of the circle.

Captain Nemo had come over to the *Saint-Michel III* and was looking at the chart shaking his head. "Your position and circle are correctly placed, Mr. Holmes. But you are right, there is no land anywhere in that circle. Do you think that Jules Verne could have misheard the coordinates or misunderstood what they were talking about?"

Holmes considered a moment before replying, "I really don't know Jules Verne all that well. Only by reputation, actually. But he is noted for being very detail minded and quite specific in his writing. If he states that the base of this group is within 75 nautical miles of this position," and he pointed to a position on the chart, "then I believe that it is somewhere within this circle. We just need to know how to look for it. I am skilled in seeing the unseen. Give me a moment to reflect on this."

As Holmes deliberated the question, a crew member came out of the cabin with a small bucket of fish. "Here you go Dr. Watson. You can give the fish to the dolphins, as that one seems to have taken a liking to you."

I thought to myself, if drenching me with cold seawater is taking a liking, I would hate to see it upset with someone. I took the bucket of fish and moved closer to the railing to look over the side. The dolphins were still keeping pace with us, and the playful dolphin seemed to be watching the deck of the ship as it leaned its body to the left so that one eye was looking in our direction. I carefully picked up a few fish trying to avoid getting the smelly fish scales all over my hand, and tossed them to the dolphins. The dolphin swimming furthest away caught a fish and swallowed it whole, while the nearer dolphin caught a fish and with a snap of its head tossed it right back at me. Without thinking, I reacted quickly and caught the fish, with a loud splat, ending up with a whole hand full of slimy fish scales. I am not sure who laughed more, the crew members snickering loudly, or the dolphin that was making a squeaking sound that sounded like a high pitched laughter.

This was too much already. I dumped the remainder of the fish over the side, dropped the bucket on the deck, and turned to wash the scaly mess off my hands. Suddenly, fish started landing all around me. The playful dolphin was catching the fish, and flipping them back on to the yacht. I had to duck several times to avoid being hit with them. I had no idea why it was behaving in this way, as I had no previous experience with dolphins. I turned back to the railing and out of frustration leaned over and shouted, "What's wrong with you? Don't you like fish?" As I was in the process of leaning over, the dolphin again made a spectacular leap, this time directly at me. As I lunged backward to avoid a collision, I lost my hat, and the dolphin grabbed it and swam away from the *Nautilus* and *Saint-Michel III*. "My Hat!" I exclaimed. "That fish just stole my hat!"

Sherlock looked up from the chart he had been studying and pointed out, "Dolphins are technically not fish, Watson. They are mammals and very intelligent mammals at that. This particular one seems to be having great sport with you."

The dolphin had swam ahead and off to the left of our course and was sticking its head out of the water and waving my hat as if to say, "Here I am. Try and catch me if you want your hat back." It swam towards the two craft and then away to the left several times repeating the action. Holmes observed the behavior intently and stated, "Watson, that dolphin with the white marking is communicating with us. Its behavior conforms expressly to the examples I included in my recent study, *"An Annotated Guide to Nonvocal Mammalian Communication Behavior, with an Emphasis on Indicating a Desired Direction of Travel"*. It wants us to turn to the left."

Captain Nemo had also been observing it and agreed. "It certainly does look that way, Mr. Holmes, but do we have the time go off on a wild dolphin chase? Who knows why it is acting this way? It could just be naturally playful."

Holmes shook his head. "I don't think so, Captain. It intentionally tried to maneuver Watson into a position where it could get a hold of his hat, something that we would need to retrieve and have to follow it to recover. I say that we should follow it. This may sound strange, but Jules Verne's letter did mention that an unidentified 'Luna', may be helpful. Unless you know of someone else that he knew named Luna, that dolphin clearly has a crescent moon shaped mark on it, and 'Luna' translates to 'moon'. It is my deduction, therefore, that this dolphin is the 'Luna' that Verne is referring to, and I say that we should follow it to where it is leading us."

Now I was really beside myself. By this time, I was soaking wet with my hand full of slimy, smelly, fish scales, and my hat, which by now was certainly ruined, was clutched in the teeth of an overly playful dolphin. First we get kidnapped onto a fictional submarine that turned out to be real, then we were whisked off on a mission to save another missing author, and now we had to go chasing after a wild dolphin. What was next, a 'giant squid attack?'

Just then, one of the crew members pointed out over the starboard side of the vessel and called out, "Giant squid off the stern quarter, Captain! What are your orders?"

Captain Nemo, Holmes, and I all turned at once to see a massive cephalopod at the surface of the waves five hundred yards astern of us with its tentacles waving wildly. It was nearly the length of Verne's former vessel, and it looked like it could easily crush the ship in its large tentacles.

Holmes pointed out that, no matter what happened, we needed to follow that dolphin, and with Captain Nemo hurriedly ran across the gang plank to the *Nautilus* calling out, "Quick Watson, come over here. We can follow the dolphin easier from the *Nautilus*. Wave at it, or something, so it knows you're on this vessel and not the steam yacht."

Trying to keep one eye on the dolphin and one on the approaching giant squid, I raced across the gang plank to the *Nautilus*, where I stopped and waved at the dolphin who surprisingly flipped my ruined hat back to me. It seemed to know that we were going to follow it, so it no longer needed the hat. I quickly went below while the crew took down the guy lines and plank in preparation for submerging. I immediately went to the large circular window and pulled the lever to spin open the metal iris where I looked to see if could find Luna the dolphin. To my surprise, it was not far from the side of the *Nautilus*, repeating its action of swimming towards us and then away to the left.

Sherlock pointed out the window, saying, "There's that behavior again, we must follow it to the left." There was a rush of bubbles as the *Nautilus* descended beneath the surface of the waves and picked up speed turning to the direction the dolphin apparently wanted us to travel. Captain Nemo entered the salon and informed us that the *Saint-Michel III* was safely making good speed away from the squid in the other direction and that it did not appear that the monstrous creature was following us. "I am sorry gentlemen, but following this dolphin is a higher priority, so you will have to wait until another time to try my outstanding recipe for Marinated Giant Squid Tentacles. It really is excellent.

And giant squid are so hard to come by these days. Tis a pity."

Looking at the puddle of salt water at my feet, Captain Nemo added, "You may want to change your clothes, Dr. Watson. I will have a crew member bring you a set of dry clothing. You wouldn't want to catch cold. Not to mention, that is a 100 year old Persian rug you are standing on."

Sherlock tilted his head to the side looking at the carpet and added, "Looking at that rug and based on my research, *"A Comprehensive Report on the Manufacture of Persian Rugs from the Fourth Century Through Current Times"*, I believe it is actually 103 years, 2 months, and 22 days old. It was completed on a Wednesday during the waxing phase of the moon, and I can tell you the name of the weaver who made it, if you are interested, but it is 27 letters long and difficult to pronounce.

I shook my head and replied, "Just get me some dry clothes please."

Chapter 5. A Most Unusual Discovery, (And who would have ever imagined it?)

I had received a spare crew uniform and was finally warm and dry. A crew member offered me a cup of seaweed tea, stating that to appreciate its full flavor and get the most benefit from it, I may want to let it steep a bit more. I looked at the exceptionally thick, dark green beverage, and mentioned to him that from what it looked like, if it was any steeper, I would need mountain climbing gear to drink it, but he apparently did not find it amusing. "Suit yourself", he replied as he set it down rather roughly. It turned out my comment was fully justified in that when he set it down, the impact of the tea cup on the table split the china cup in two with the pieces falling away from the tea, while the tea retained its shape and form remaining quite solid almost as if it were a gel. Needless to say, I decided to forgo the tea.

With the unbelievable speed of the *Nautilus*, we had traveled quite some distance while I was changing clothes and getting dried off. During that time, Sherlock had created a message to send out to the Atlantean network, one person at a time, along with instructions to the communications officer how to determine where the compromise in their network had taken place. Our dolphin friend, Luna, had continued to indicate the direction of travel the entire time, but now she seemed to be circling. Captain Nemo gave the command to bring the *Nautilus* to a full stop, and we hung there suspended in the endless liquid environment, gazing out into the undersea world and wondering what was to be our next move.

Looking out one of the large circular viewing windows, Captain Nemo asked, "Now what do you propose? It appears that this is where the dolphin wants to take us, but I don't notice anything out of the ordinary. Let us initiate a slow circle of the vicinity to determine what it is Luna is trying to show us."

Captain Nemo issued a command into the speaking tube, and the vessel commenced a slow circular path as we peered out through the two viewing ports, not knowing what specifically we were looking for. The sea floor looked normal enough to me, not that I had ever seen it before that day. The colors faded from a deep azure blue, to purple, and then, to darkness. Sherlock stared intently out the viewing port and expounded, "What we are looking for is what should not be there, even if it is disguised as something that should be there. If only I had a copy of my paper, *"A Guide to Seeing the Unseen by Observing the*

Cleary Invisible yet Obviously Visible to the Trained Eye", you would clearly understand what I am talking about."

Sherlock turned his head as if a thought had suddenly struck him and asked, "How far have we traveled from the point mentioned in Verne's message? And how far were we from that point when we decoded the message?"

Captain Nemo checked a chart that was on one of the tables in the salon, performed several calculations and confirmed we were within the area identified by Verne as the possible location for the base of Verne's captors.

Sherlock continued staring out the viewing point while he answered, "I am certain that we will find something out there related to Jules Verne's disappearance. It is just a matter of seeing the unseen."

Captain Nemo suddenly pointed to a location outside the port viewing window and asked, "What about the clearly visible, yet completely out of place? Do you see that sperm whale there? The depth of this location is entirely too shallow for sperm whales. They are a deep water species. You would never find one at this depth. And it seems as if it is just sitting on the ocean floor. That is very unnatural behavior. I have spent decades observing marine life in its natural habitat, and I have never seen anything like this before."

We gathered around the viewing port to see what Captain Nemo was referring to, and there sitting motionless on the ocean floor was a medium sized sperm whale. It was very bulky and long, and while it looked similar to the illustrations of sperm whales that I had seen in books in the past, there was something that seemed unnatural about it. It was almost too perfect.

"Look at it!", declared Holmes, "There are no scratch marks anywhere on its body. In every illustration of a sperm whale that I have ever seen, they are covered with scrapes and scratches from encounters with squid or other marine life. That creature hasn't a mark on its body. How would you explain that for a whale of this size, Captain Nemo?"

The Captain shook his head as he responded, "I can't. There is no natural explanation for that. The only possibility I can think of is that it is not a real whale. It's a fabrication. It is very realistic and natural looking, and from afar, it would fool most anyone. But seeing it this close and so clearly underwater, the perfection of it shatters the illusion."

"But why would anyone create an imitation sperm whale?" I asked. "What would be the purpose of such a creation? Do you think it could be a submersible vessel disguised as a whale? That there might be people inside that thing?"

The *Nautilus* was positioned directly across from it now with less than 100 yards between us and the mysterious creature. The skin was smooth and lifelike, but as Holmes had pointed out, it looked almost new, as if it had just been created. Suddenly there was a profusion of air bubbles around the whale, and it quickly bolted forward from its position with its tale rapidly flipping up and down in a movement that was more mechanical than natural. The eyes of the whale had a glow to them as if there was a light source behind them. In just a moment, it was out of the area covered by the viewing window, but the crew in the control room had a longer viewing range from the two forward-looking ports. They reported that the ship, or creature, or whatever it was, had executed a wide turn and was coming directly towards us at a very fast speed. Captain Nemo issued several commands into the speaking tube and told us to hold on to something. Just as the whale was nearing us and a collision seemed imminent, the *Nautilus* executed a very sharp turn that nearly pitched us on our sides. If the aquariums on the shelves had not been sealed, they certainly would have spilled their contents. Dishes and some of the food from the table were thrown to the floor as the artificial whale slid past us missing the *Nautilus* by the smallest margin. Nemo issued another command, and the *Nautilus* surged forward at full speed away from the strange creation.

The captain looked at the ruined food and commented, "That was the last of our sautéed octopus that just landed on the floor of the salon. They are going to pay for that. Are they following us?" A crew member informed us that the whale had again made a turn and was indeed following us as fast as it could, but the *Nautilus* could easily outrun it, if the Captain so desired. Nemo informed the crewman that he wanted to stay just out of reach of it and issued a course heading, adding that if it worked out as he planned, we would be in for quite a sight.

As the *Nautilus* raced through the undersea world with the strange creature following us, Holmes having observed the creature the entire time stated, "Captain Nemo, in examining the motion and behavior of that 'whale' I can see that is most certainly a submersible vessel disguised as whale. What is your plan?"

The Captain had been briefly looking at a chart when he exclaimed, "It should be... right about... now!" As Captain Nemo finished his statement, he pointed out the viewing port to a spot up ahead and cried out, "There! That is what I was looking for, the giant squid that we saw earlier, I had hoped it would still be somewhere in the vicinity where we left it. Observe!"

The giant squid was indeed still in the area where he had expected it to be and it was even more terrifying to see its full length underwater. The tentacles were covered with hundreds of circular suction cups surrounded by tiny serrated teeth, and the parrot like beak was not something I would want to encounter first hand. Thankfully, the squid paid   no attention to the *Nautilus* and maneuvered straight towards the artificial sperm whale. It is well known that the giant squid and sperm whale are natural enemies with the whales typically feeding on the squid, but my guess is that Captain Nemo hoped that, given the opportunity and its immense size, this particular squid would take the role of the aggressor and distract the whale submersible.

Sherlock pointed and interjected, "I see your plan, Captain. It appears to be working. The squid went right for the whale." Indeed, the cephalopod had wrapped its tentacles around the fabricated whale, and had rendered the mechanical tale inoperable. Bits of artificial skin were being ripped off the whale in the struggle, revealing a metal structure beneath it. "But what about the people inside the craft?" Sherlock pointed out. "It is possible that Jules Verne may be held prisoner in there. We can't let the squid destroy the vessel."

Captain Nemo issued a command into the communication tube and responded, "That is true, Mr. Holmes. Please observe." The *Nautilus* closed the distance between ourselves, and the squid and whale submersible that were locked in terrible combat. The helmsman brought the hull of the *Nautilus* into contact with the body of the massive cephalopod. There was a bright blue flash as the exterior surface of the submersible delivered a strong electrical shock to the squid, which promptly released the whale and retreated from the area leaving a dark cloudy trail as cephalopods do when they wish to hide. The Captain watched as the giant squid vanished into the murky blue distance and commented, "That could have been an excellent meal of marinated giant squid tentacles."

The tale flipper mechanism of the whale had been badly damaged during the battle with the squid, so the craft no longer posed a ramming threat, but we still had to find out who was inside it. A rush of air bubbles indicated that it was rising to the surface, and the *Nautilus* followed suit. As both vessels broke the surface, the *Nautilus*'s crew immediately secured lines to the mystery vessel and, armed with strange looking rifles, looked for some sort of access to the interior. There was a distinct mechanical sound from inside, and a section in the upper back portion of the whale's head opened up to reveal an entrance to the interior of the mysterious vessel.

Sherlock, Captain Nemo, and I climbed the stairs up to the deck of the *Nautilus* to observe the proceedings, and Holmes pointed out, "If you look closely, you can see where that hatch was designed to be nearly invisible when closed. My deduction is that this vessel is pneumatically powered by the use of compressed air cylinders. That would explain the mechanical motion of the tail propulsion, and the air bubbles. This is a very clever creation." Pointing towards the hatch, Sherlock drew our attention to several figures emerging with hands held up in surrender. "Look! They are exiting the craft. It appears that they are surrendering, but if they have any type of wireless communication device similar to that used by your Atlantean network and you take them aboard the *Nautilus*, that could be a way for their organization to track them and in doing so, track us. That would let their leaders know where we are. I suggest the prisoners be searched for any device that could be used in such a way, and if you are able to call your crew aboard Jules Verne's yacht; have them return to the area. The prisoners can be detained on board the *Saint-Michel III*.

Captain Nemo gave a command to his crew members guarding the individuals who had exited the craft. The three were all of medium build with dark hair and thin mustaches, wore dark colored uniforms and tall boots. They spoke accented English and explained that their submersible whale vessel had been severely damaged and would not stay afloat for long. They offered their surrender in exchange for safety.

Sherlock told Captain Nemo that he needed to see the interior of the vessel before it sank and entered the hatch calling for me to follow. Stepping through a hatchway into a vessel that one knows is about to sink is not something I would recommend to the claustrophobic or faint of heart or one who is overly concerned for their safety or, for that matter, anyone at all. Nevertheless, I followed Holmes into the dark recess below the hatch. Ignoring the creaks and groans of the foundering vessel, the rising water at his feet, and the sparks emitting from the control panels on the walls of the cramped interior, Sherlock stood in rapt fascination at the design and workmanship of the craft. "This is quite impressive, Watson! There is some very advanced design work here. I shall have to update my paper on *"Proposed Practical Applications and Logical Usage of Pneumatics in Transportation."*

Concerned with the water level and stability of the vessel, I hurriedly replied, "That's if we get out of here in time. What exactly are we looking for, Holmes?"

Sherlock quickly responded, "Anything that would tell us if Jules Verne has been aboard this vessel. Luna led us directly to this craft. There must have been some reason for that behavior. I believe we will find our next clue somewhere here if we can locate it before the vessel sinks."

Sherlock and I had experienced many short deadlines when looking for clues in the past. I can remember times when we had less than eight hours to find some clue or proof to prevent an innocent man from being executed. In this case, we had mere minutes to find some unknown bit of evidence before we lost our own lives. What could it be? The interior of the vessel was quite small and crowded with equipment, air tanks, and lines. There were assorted odds and ends everywhere, and the water was rising higher and higher by the second. Sherlock had gone into the forward compartment, and was I am sure, using his unequaled skill in perception, when suddenly, the amount of water coming from the stern of the whale shaped vessel increased dramatically and the back end began to tilt downward.

"Sherlock!" I cried. "We have got to get out of here!" I had hurried back up through the hatch and turned to be certain he was following me, when a rush of water burst out of the hatch and the vessel started to settle below the surface. The only things holding it up were the lines that held it to the *Nautilus*. Captain Nemo's crew was urging me to come back to the *Nautilus* before I would be pulled under by the suction of the sinking vessel. The interior of the craft was now completely full of water, and it seemed hopeless, but I was determined not lose my best friend and the world's most talented consulting detective. I was about to dive into the hatch to make one last attempt to find him, when the strangest creature began to climb out of the hatch. I stepped back, not knowing what it was, as it appeared to be some sort of giant sea shell with tubes and a mechanical valve mounted on it. As it continued to exit, I saw that it was not a 'creature', but it was Sherlock wearing some type of underwater breathing device over his head, air supply on his back, and holding a pocket watch in his hand. We quickly returned to the deck of the *Nautilus*, after which Nemo's crew cut the lines that supported the sperm whale vessel, and it returned to the depths for the last time.

As Sherlock removed the breathing device, I exclaimed, "Holmes, you gave me such a start! I thought you had drowned in there. How did you know what that contraption is much less what to do with it? And why did you risk your life just to retrieve a pocket watch?"

"If you look at this piece of equipment Watson, you will see it cannot be anything but a cleverly designed underwater breathing device. It uses a very large sea shell to hold the air and delivers it via hoses to the helmet. You do recall that paper I wrote *"On Determining the Functionality and Purpose of Unknown Objects in Less Than Three Seconds Using Rational Deductive Observation"*. Once you identify an object, it is quite simple to deduce how it works. I knew I would be able to use it to extend my time to search the forward cabin. While I did not find Jules Verne, I did find this."

As he spoke, Sherlock set the breathing apparatus and helmet down on the deck and held up the watch so I could clearly see the initials engraved into the back of the watch case, "J.G.V."

Chapter 6. A Most Unusual Lead, (But certainly rather timely.)

Sherlock had found a watch with initials that matched those of Jules Gabriel Verne. It was a lead which quite possibly proved that Verne had been aboard the whale submersible, but now what were we to do, since the strange craft had sank and taken with it any additional clues? As we spoke, a steam auxiliary was seen approaching from the West, and I commented, "That looks like Jules Verne's former steam yacht."

Captain Nemo confirmed my observation. "It is, Dr. Watson. We are going to deposit the captured crewmen on board the *Saint-Michel III*, so there is no chance of them in any way broadcasting our position to their leaders. According to them, they are just paid crew members on an experimental craft, and they were separated from the main vessel, which was observing the whale submersible's operation. They claim to know nothing at all about Jules Verne or his whereabouts."

Sherlock replied, "I don't need to talk to them to know that they are lying. This watch tells more than just time. It is also a message from Jules Verne himself. When your prisoners are removed from the *Nautilus*, please do meet me in the salon of your vessel, and I will explain. And by the way, do you happen to have a copy of Jules Verne's book, "*A Journey to the Center of the Earth?*"

Captain Nemo replied there was a first edition copy in the *Nautilus* library located in the salon and that he would be along momentarily. As we descended into the interior of Nemo's vessel, I wondered, how a simple pocket watch could be a 'message' from Jules Verne and why Holmes had asked about a copy of Verne's famous underground adventure. As soon as we reentered the luxurious room that contained Captain Nemo's library, Sherlock immediately went over to the bookshelves and retrieved a copy of Verne's novel. He then made his way to a table and set the watch and book down next to each other. "Now, I could use a writing implement, some ink, and some paper," he said aloud, to which I simply handed them to him, as he had left the items on the table where he had previously been working on the translation of the Atlantean language. Of course, since we were aboard the *Nautilus*, the ink was squid based, as one would expect.

"What are you doing Sherlock?" I asked quite bluntly. "What is so special about this watch?"

Sherlock clicked open the case of the pocket watch and pointed to the inside of the cover and simply replied, "This! It is a message from Jules Verne."

There were a number of very tiny marks scratched into the inside of the metal cover of the watch. They looked like no more than random scratching to me, more like a bird had been pecking on it, or perhaps the watch case had been left open while carried in a pocket full of sharp rocks or nails.

"And what is the significance of those markings?" I asked. "They don't look very important as far as I can see."

With his usual frankness, Sherlock replied, "That is because you don't see very far, Watson." Leafing through the copy of *"A Journey to the Center of the Earth"*, Sherlock continued, "You do remember that monograph I wrote a few years ago, *"Cryptology, Ciphers, Codes, and Secret Languages and How to Determine Their Hidden Meaning"*. I knew what this was as soon as I spotted it, but to read it, I needed a copy of this." He had opened Verne's book to the page that displayed the cipher that a character in the book, Arnie Saknusum, had used to hide a secret message. It had been written in Viking runic characters as well as in code and was a key point in the novel. Sherlock began copying the markings from the watch case and then used the runic cipher to translate the message. After only a moment, he set down the writing implement, and declared to Captain Nemo, who had just entered, "It's just as I suspected. Jules Verne was able to leave us a clue as to where they are taking him. This message contains the coordinates of the location they are headed to. We must alter our course immediately, Captain." Sherlock held out the paper that contained the course heading. Nemo took the information from Holmes and handed it to a crew member with instructions to adjust the course. Turning to Sherlock, he asked, "Did you find anything else of interest inside the vessel before it sank?"

Sherlock paused for a moment before answering, "Next to the *Nautilus*, that submersible was more advanced than anything any of the European nations have built to date. The French submersible *Piongeur* and the Spanish *Icentio II* were positively primitive compared to what I saw down there. The question is: Where did they get their technology? It is not at the level of your *Nautilus*, but it is still years ahead of the rest of the world. I am certain that the science of your *Nautilus* has been kept secret over the years, so that could not be the source."

Captain Nemo shook his head and affirmed Holmes' comment. "I assure you that the technology of the *Nautilus* has remained hidden from all except Jules Verne. That is why we need to rescue him as quickly as possible. Even in his novel, he did not explain the true nature and functionality of the power source of the *Nautilus*. He did an excellent job of telling an engaging story without giving away any important details. Where they acquired their science is beyond my grasp at this time."

"Where are we headed now?" I interrupted. "What is our next destination?"

Captain Nemo spread out the chart on which had been drawn the circle within which the home base of the mysterious group was located. "We are here," he stated, pointing towards two positions on the chart, "and we are headed here. It should not take us long. Again, there is nothing on the chart to indicate that there is an island or land of any kind in that location."

Sherlock, however, raised a question. "But what if they do not need dry land? What if their base is located on a seamount? An undersea mountain that never broke the surface of the ocean? Or perhaps an ancient volcano that has subsided to a depth below the surface of the ocean. If they have the technology to create that whale vessel, then it is only logical that they have also mastered the science of underwater living structures. They would be invisible to the rest of the world, much like you and your *Nautilus*. With their submersibles disguised as whales, they could go to and from their base without anyone noticing. And with that location, they could be a serious threat to shipping in the English Channel, especially if they have knowledge of advanced science and weapons from the future. How much does Jules Verne actually know of future technology at this time?"

The captain exhaled deeply. "Based on his writings, 100 years from now, Jules Verne will most likely be known as the man who predicted the future. He knows quite a bit, but in a more general way, as opposed to specific details. Still, he would not purposely divulge information to those who would misuse it. Nevertheless, I fear for his safety."

While they were talking, my gaze wandered toward the large circular viewing port, and I happened to spot Luna swimming alongside the *Nautilus*. As I watched her swim, the strangest thing occurred. I cannot say if it was an after effect of the seaweed tea I had tried earlier or a side effect of the air on board or perhaps something else entirely. I was not paying any attention to the dolphin. She was just in my peripheral vision outside of my main focal point when, for a moment, she appeared not as a dolphin but as a mermaid, swimming outside the viewing port. As impossible as it seems, for that brief second, she appeared to be a real mermaid with long, flowing dark hair, a strikingly beautiful face, the bluest eyes I had ever seen, and yes, a luminous green, scaly fish tail. She wore a metallic blue colored top that accentuated her lovely form. The vision lasted only a second, for when I focused more directly on Luna, I was looking at a dolphin again. Yet, I could not shake the picture of the mermaid I had seen, from my mind. I knew it was simply not possible. I would have dismissed it as just my imagination getting the better of me, but the crescent moon mark had been clearly visible on the nymph's forehead, and I would have sworn she had looked at me and smiled.

Now, Sherlock has stated many times that eye witnesses are the worst evidence for a case, as the human eye can be so easily deceived, and the human mind can so readily misinterpret what it thinks it sees. One client was positive his wife was a vampire. Another was certain his family was cursed and that a demon dog was after him. Sherlock was easily able to disprove these cases, yet the clients were absolutely positive of what they thought they had seen. This had to be a simple case of misreading what I saw and nothing more. I would certainly not mention it to Holmes.

Chapter 7. A Most Unusual Sight,
(So there is some truth to that old tale.)

I had no sooner determined that what I had seen was an illusion resulting from, perhaps, fatigue, when again Luna briefly appeared to me as a mermaid. This time I was staring directly at her. One moment I was looking at Luna the dolphin, and the next moment, a mermaid was right outside the viewing port. This time there was no mistaking what I was seeing. She was extraordinary and beguiling as well! I quickly called to Holmes and Captain Nemo to look out the viewing port, and when they did, Sherlock commented, "Ah yes, it is Luna the dolphin. She is still out there, I see. That creature exhibits a strong intelligence. Eh, Watson? I wonder why it is that she continues to follow us."

Captain Nemo remained silent for a moment and stared at me before replying, "Why indeed? Yes, dolphins are quite intelligent. But then, the sea has many mysteries and things we cannot explain. I am sure you will experience more of these mysteries before our journey is over."

Now what did Captain Nemo mean by that? Did he know something about Luna that he was not saying? Was I really seeing a mermaid out there? But that could not be possible. Everyone knows mermaids are an old sailor's legend. I turned from the viewing port to focus my attention on the conversation between Captain Nemo and Holmes, but my thoughts kept drifting back to Luna as Captain Nemo addressed Sherlock. "So Mr. Holmes, if we do find an underwater base at this location what do you suggest?

Holmes thoughtfully replied, "Well, that depends a great deal on what we find. I would suggest that we approach the location with extreme caution and perhaps stop before we get to the destination. Is it possible to send an underwater scouting party to reconnoiter the vicinity? Jules Verne's novel described underwater breathing equipment and that whale submersible had the breathing device that I used to escape, so I deduce that you do have such equipment aboard the *Nautilus*. We do not know their weaponry or the extent of what they…"

Once again, my thoughts were drifting back to the mystery of Luna and the mermaid. What was I truthfully seeing out there? I had already experienced a considerable amount of strange creatures and literary characters coming to life in our previous adventure, but there was a somewhat, sort of, possible logical explanation for it all. Perhaps Lewis Carroll's agreement and wager with the Time Guardians had somehow brought it all about. But mermaids? Impossible! They simply did not exist! That was it. Final! Finished! The end! No more discussion. If I looked out that viewing port again, I would see a dolphin named "Luna". No questions asked!

Of course, when I looked out the port I saw the alluring mermaid again, this time looking straight at me with the most dazzling, deepest eyes I had ever beheld. Her smile was radiant and mesmerizing. She was overwhelmingly captivating. This time I did not turn away. Truthfully, I could not turn away. She had enchanted me completely and unconditionally. I was hers forever. I continued to stare until, from what seemed like a far away distance, I heard Holmes asking me a question. "Isn't that right Watson? What do you think?"

I blinked and once again there was Luna where the mermaid had been swimming. "What was that, Sherlock? I wasn't paying attention there for just a moment. Could you repeat the question? I don't think I am feeling quite well."

Sherlock looked at me curiously. "Indeed, Watson, pull yourself together. You look as if you have seen a mermaid or something. The captain was asking if you want to be part of the underwater scouting team, and I was saying, after all we went through in our previous adventure, nothing would bother you. But I am beginning to wonder about that. Are you feeling ill? Maybe you could use a cup of the medicinal seaweed tea."

"No thank you!" I replied rather abruptly. I was not in the mood for any more of a tea that one could cut with a knife, and most likely dull the knife in the process, if you did not break it out right. Yet what was he saying about going outside the *Nautilus* underwater? Maybe it would be an opportunity to see what was really going on with that dolphin or mermaid or whatever it was. I decided to accept the offer and replied, "Yes, thank you! That might be a fascinating experience. How exactly does the breathing apparatus work? What do I need to do?"

The captain escorted Sherlock and me to the airlock chamber of the vessel and gave us instructions on the use of his underwater breathing equipment. It was quite remarkable. The system was similar to the one that Sherlock had used to escape the whale submersible, but instead of a large sea shell to hold the air, it was comprised of a compressed air tank with hoses that were attached to a helmet that fastened to the collar of a suit that was made of a water-tight material. There was a belt with weights and metal shoes to prevent us from being too buoyant. He explained that with the air in the tank, we should have one hour of breathing time and to make sure we did not stray too far from the *Nautilus*. Attached to the wrist of the underwater suit was a watch that had been specially treated to be water-tight.

We had safely arrived at a place near our final destination but hidden from view behind a large rock outcropping covered with kelp and other seaweed. The Captain also gave Sherlock a special type of rifle of his own design that worked underwater and fired an electrically charged bolt. I hoped he would not have to use it. My thoughts were wholly on Luna and the mermaid. Was the dolphin actually a mermaid? How on earth could that be possible? Whatever the case turned out to be, I looked forward to receiving my answer soon.

The *Nautilus* had come to rest on the ocean floor out of sight of the seamount. Sherlock and I were to be accompanied by Captain Nemo and two of his crew members. He explained that we would be able to communicate with each other with the full helmets, which gave us not only air to breathe, but also a medium in which to speak. We would, however, need to be in close range to hear each other. Sherlock remarked that this experience would provide an excellent basis for the paper he was writing *"On Communication in Atmospheres and Mediums of Varying Densities and Determining Maximum Audible Range"*. He cheerfully added, "This will be quite the experience, eh, Watson old boy! I imagine this underwater expedition will be even more exciting than our little jaunts courtesy of H. G. Wells' Time Machine."

"Exciting" was not the adjective I would have used for those trips, and I hoped that our underwater excursion would not be, in any way similar. We had barely escaped with our lives from that bit of madness. Referring to those "little jaunts" as "exciting" is like saying that being blindfolded and strapped to a wild horse as it gallops down the side of an erupting volcano is equivalent to an afternoon ride in the park. "Terrifying", "alarming", or "death defying" would be a more suitable description for that experience.

But now I was trying to focus on what I was about to do. I was going to step out of a perfectly safe and dry underwater vessel into a liquid environment that could kill me in a dozen different ways in seconds, using breathing equipment that I had never seen before, much less used. What was I thinking? Sherlock and

Captain Nemo had already exited the vessel through a large hatch in the bottom of the floor of the air chamber room that opened into a pool of water. I was standing on the edge of the pool wondering what on earth I was doing, and why was I doing it, when one of the crewmen urged me forward and I stepped off the edge into the watery blue abyss. I was sure my life was over.

It was beyond belief! I slowly sunk to the sea bottom several feet below the open hatch in the *Nautilus*. I rapidly reached the ocean floor, raising a cloud of silt, and Sherlock grabbed my arm to move me out of the way of the remaining crew members who would be dropping from the hatch to accompany us. What an unbelievable experience! I was underwater and breathing! Even more miraculous, I was still alive. In spite of the water-tight suit, I felt chilled from the seawater that surrounded me with its frigid cold embrace. I gazed around me and noticed a wide variety of fish and other marine life, but I did not see Luna anywhere. I was still in the vicinity of Captain Nemo, Sherlock, and the crew members who had also descended to the ocean floor, so that could explain Luna's absence. Captain Nemo took the lead and indicated the direction we were to travel. While the equipment and weighted shoes had been cumbersome on board the *Nautilus*, it was easier to move about underwater due to the buoyancy. Still it was so foreign and strange to be walking on the ocean floor. It was almost intoxicating. We carefully made our way towards the seamount wondering what we would find there. As we made our way forward, I continued to look for signs of Luna, but without success. Captain Nemo abruptly held up his hand to stop our scouting group and then pointed to the seamount on the right. Upon the undersea plateau was a small underwater compound.

Several interconnected metal structures covered with a multitude of pipes and valves were located on the surface of the seamount. There were hatches on the sides of them which were most likely air locks similar to the chamber I had just used to exit the *Nautilus*. A docking platform was resting on pilings located on top of one of the structures. A second even larger platform seemed to be some type of elevator that could be raised to the ocean surface. This must be a base of operations. How could we possibly gain access to the interior without being noticed? I did not think it would be possible, when I heard Sherlock explain his plan to Captain Nemo. "It is really quite simple, Captain. They must have a power source to maintain their presence here and some type of apparatus to maintain their air supply. If you look over there, I would say that is the air system purifier for the entire base. Send your crew back to the *Nautilus* to get a concentrated quantity of the seaweed tea that you tried to drug us with, and have them put it under pressure using one of your breathing cylinders. I can add it to their air supply and render the whole base unconscious. Then we can slip inside undetected to see what we can find."

As we waited for the crew to return, I was in awe at Holmes' deductive ability. He had just glanced at a complex structure based on science far beyond anything of our time and unquestionably known what to do. While we were waiting, I also took advantage of the opportunity to look around the vicinity to see if Luna was still nearby. I could not get the irresistible vision of her out of my mind and was determined to get an answer. The underwater visibility was somewhat limited, so I could not see very far. I decided to take a few steps away to see further into the murky blue depths when suddenly the mermaid appeared directly in front of me! She put one hand on my shoulder and one finger to her lip to indicate, "Don't say a word." She really did not need to caution me, as I was utterly speechless. I blinked my eyes several times, and she was still before me. This time, there was no question or doubting. The mermaid was real. How would I ever explain this to Holmes? It was not logical. But logical or not, she was there and pulling on my arm to move me further away from where Sherlock and Captain Nemo were waiting. With each motion of her scaly, green tail, the distance increased. Not knowing what to do, I gave in, and let her lead the way and she pointed to an underwater cave opening in the rock formation. With a flip of her tail she disappeared into the cave entrance and then immediately reappeared urging me to follow her.

As I entered the undersea cavern, I noticed that the sea floor sloped upward, and soon I was breaking the surface of the water inside the chamber which contained an air pocket. It was medium in size, and the ceiling which disappeared into darkness above me, was covered in sparkling crystalline cave formations, while the bottom consisted of a ledge that surrounded a small pool of water. I made my way over to the ledge to sit down, as I was overwhelmed by the complete strangeness of everything. In a moment, she had burst out of the pool and was sitting by my side with her tail still in the water and her hands clutching my arms as she pleaded with me to listen. I have to say that seeing her so close in her true mermaid appearance made it quite a challenge not to sit and dumbfoundedly stare at her. Any true English gentleman would tell you it is simply not proper. In spite of her intoxicating beauty, I did manage to avoid staring and listened intently to what she was urgently saying. She pleaded, "Sir, you must listen to me. Your life depends on it. If you are trying to save Monsieur Verne, you and your friends must not enter that structure. It is a trap! He was there, but they have taken him away in a flying machine. If anyone enters any one of those metal boxes, the air chamber doorways will be destroyed along with whoever is nearby. I heard them planning it. They know they are being followed and are willing to sacrifice their base to stop you. I will explain everything in more detail later, but you must stop your friends from going in there. Go! Go quickly!" And with that, she dove into the water pulling me with her and pushing me back out of the cave, when suddenly, the sound of a nearby explosion shook the area.

Chapter 8. A Most Unusual Turn of Events,
(But of course, Sherlock saw it coming.)

A feeling of dread and fear overwhelmed me. We were too late! While I was distracted by the mermaid, they had tried to enter the compound and had triggered the trap. Sherlock and the others were probably dead or seriously injured. Trying to see through the cloud of sediment that had been raised by the explosion, I hurried back to where I had left them and was relieved to see them still alive and well gathered behind the rock formation. How was it possible? I moved close enough to Sherlock to be able to communicate and asked him, "Holmes, how did you know about the explosives attached to the entry hatches?" To which he replied, "Watson, where have you been? And how did YOU know about the explosives attached to the entry hatches?

I was about to tell him when Captain Nemo motioned for Sherlock to move forward, and asked him to check for any additional explosives. Holmes nodded and stated, "Don't be concerned. I will verify it is safe. This is unequivocally what I covered in my monograph, *"An Analytical Approach to Detecting Hidden Bombs, Booby traps, and Explosive Devices in All Situations with an Emphasis on Doorways"*. Give me just a moment."

Without waiting for my reply, Sherlock strode forward to the structures trailing behind him a thin rope line. Captain Nemo explained to me Sherlock had spotted the hidden explosives on the entry hatch while he was attaching the drugged gas to their air supply and that he had detonated the explosive using a trip line from behind the safety of the rock formation. He also asked me how I had known about the trap when I was not in the area when Holmes had discovered it. I turned to point out the mermaid, but she had again disappeared. I did not know what to think or what to say to the Captain. Fortunately, I did not have to answer as Sherlock returned to the shelter of the rocks trailing the line.

"It is as I expected. There was a second trap on the inner air chamber door. Brace yourselves!"

And with that, he pulled on the line, and there was a second explosion. When the turbulence ceased, Sherlock told us to wait while he investigated further. Nemo and his crew were looking in the direction of Sherlock as he trudged back to the structures, when I felt a hand on my shoulder and heard Luna's voice against the back of my breathing helmet. "Your friend is in danger. There is one more trap that he will not see. We must stop him!" And suddenly my arm was in the grasp of a dolphin that was quickly dragging me towards Sherlock with each flip of her powerful tail fin. Just as Sherlock was about to re-enter the structure, I grabbed his arm, pulling him into voice range and cautioning him, "Wait Holmes, don't go in. There is one more trap that you would not see!"

When I had pulled him away from the door, Luna, still in her dolphin appearance, quickly swam up to the chamber entrance carrying a piece of metal debris, which she flung into the chamber, and then swam quickly away. Just as she had reached a safe distance from the entrance, there was yet another explosion which blew open the entire chamber.

As the silt and turbulence from the detonation settled, Holmes went over to the remains of the structure and looked inside. I saw him reach in for a moment, and then he returned to where I was, leaned towards me and stated, "Let us return to the *Nautilus*. We are getting low on air and you need to explain what is going on with that dolphin and how you knew about the third explosive device without having entered the structure."

We had made our way back to the *Nautilus*, reentered the air chamber room, and were removing the underwater breathing gear when the pool of water at the entrance hatch in the bottom of the floor was broken by a large splash. First it looked as if a dolphin was jumping out of the water, but then the mermaid, burst through the surface of the pool. She gracefully sat on the edge of the pool with her iridescent scaly fish tail still hanging in the water, her long dark hair flowing over her shoulders, and a whimsical expression on her face. Her metallic blue top sparkled in the light of the airlock chamber. She smiled, looked at us, and simply stated, "Hello. My name is Luna. Yes, I really am a mermaid, and no, I am not a harbinger of storms, shipwrecks or death. I would imagine you have more than several questions. We 'shell sea', if I answer them." She then gave a playful swish of her luminous green tail.

The silence was at first overwhelming, then Captain Nemo and his crew started asking questions all at the same time, as they stared at her with wide eyes, and awestruck faces.

"How is it possible?" asked the Mate.

"Where did you come from?" the Bosun inquired.

"If you please, just where have you been hiding for the last several centuries?" The Captain politely asked.

"Are you married?" an unidentified crewman piped in, adding, "And if you are married, do you have any sisters?"

Sherlock, however, was much more practical in his approach, as he bowed slightly to her and said, "Greetings Miss Luna. Thank you so very much for your assistance. How is it that you knew of the explosive traps in the base? And what can you tell us about where they have taken Jules Verne?"

I shook my head in amazement. I have often stated that Sherlock Holmes is as unemotional as a calculating machine and as cold as a fish. Here, he had the closest thing to a talking fish sitting right in front of him, and he didn't even blink an eye. An impossibly beautiful creature of legend, lies, and myth, a genuine mermaid, was sitting right in front of him, and he talks to her like a common London resident, no different than any other person he had ever questioned.

She nodded her head back to him and answered, "My existence is a very long story, which you do not have time for at the moment. I will go into greater detail on my history later. Regarding my knowledge of their traps, in my dolphin appearance, it was easy to overhear what they were planning. No one pays attention to dolphins no matter how smart they may seem. I do know that they have a flying machine similar to what Jules Verne described in one of his books. If you bring me a navigation chart, I can direct you to the location they have taken him. It is surrounded by water, so you should not have great difficulty in reaching that place."

Then looking directly at Sherlock, she added, "You have been very creative in discovering, understanding, and following Monsieur Verne's clues as well as seeing and avoiding the enemy's hidden explosive traps."

As Captain Nemo sent a crew member to retrieve a nautical chart, Sherlock answered, "It is elementary, really. It is simply a matter of knowing correctly where to look, what specifically one should be looking for, and ignoring everything else in the vicinity. It is quite straightforward once one understands the process."

Shaking my head, I added, "And don't forget believing it when one sees it."

She turned to look at me, smiled, and replied, "That is where you have difficulty, good sir. I can tell that you have a very caring heart and a gentle soul, which is why I chose you, to communicate with. Yet still, it took me the longest time before you accepted that I was there and that I really am a mermaid. Even now you are overwhelmed by my presence. I actually find that very sweet. Returning to my dolphin appearance, people's lack of imagination and unwillingness to accept what they do not understand makes it very easy to hide in plain sight, since they do not see me as I truly appear. Sometimes, I enjoy confusing fishermen 'on porpoise'." She laughed brightly at her humor in a lilting, melodious voice and added, "But if I get nervous, I just 'clam up'." And she laughed again, this time echoing like wind chimes.

Then turning towards the chart that had been brought to her, she pointed at a spot and stated, "There! That is where they are taking him. It is a diminutive volcanic island off the coast of Iceland, deserted and rather remote. Your submersible craft can travel as nearly rapidly as their flying machine, so you can compensate for lost time, but you must be expedient."

Captain Nemo issued a command to his crew to set a course at full speed for the location Luna had indicated and commented, "If you do not mind my observation, your vocabulary is quite excellent for a mythical creature."

She gave a slight rustle of her tail and replied, "As is yours for a fictional, literary character. You are not the only one here that is older than their appearance. One can achieve an excellent vocabulary over decades of observing and listening to humans from the unnoticed vantage point of a dolphin."

Sherlock, however, interrupted the discussion to return to more practical matters. "When the current situation is resolved, you two can continue your debate on whose vocabulary is more prodigious, but for now, we must eschew that deliberation and lucubrate as much as possible on what will aid us in extricating Jules Verne. Luna, what more can you tell me about his captors? Based on what I saw at that base, I no longer believe that it was Professor Moriority. This is far beyond his capabilities. The science and technology of this organization is almost equal to that of you and your *Nautilus*, Captain Nemo. I would say that there is yet another group out there similar to the descendants of Atlantis."

Luna looked at Sherlock and stated, "It is as you observed, Mr. Holmes. The star map and initial "M" does not stand for your Professor Moriority. It stands for the survivors of the Lost City of Mu."

Sherlock pondered only a moment before replying, "The Lost City of Mu was proposed by Augustus Le Plongeon based upon his investigations of Mayan ruins in the Yucatan peninsula. He stated that the writings he had translated proved that they were much older than many other ancient civilizations. It is now a commonly-held belief that Le Plongeon actually got the name "Mu" from the French scholar and archeologist, Abbe Charles Étienne Brasseur de Bourbourg who in fact, had made a translation error while working with the Madrid Codex and a pre-Columbian Mayan script. Brasseur was positive that a word he interpreted as Mu referred to an ancient land submerged beneath the ocean. Le Plongeon then misidentified this lost land as a continent which he conjectured had sunk into the Atlantic Ocean. The general consensus among most historians, however, is that it never existed."

Surprised to hear his detailed description of Mu, I observed, "Sherlock, when did you become the expert on lost civilizations?"

He dismissively replied, "Watson, you recall last year I had to do a bit of research to recover a collection of priceless artifacts that had mysteriously disappeared from inside a locked gallery in the London Museum of Natural History. In addition to locating and returning them, I also gathered enough information to pen a small monograph on *"A Logical, Deductive Approach to the Analysis of Lost Cities, Civilizations, and Continents to Determine Their Factual Status."*

Captain Nemo raised a pointed finger and interrupted Sherlock. "That was a detailed definition of the Lost City of Mu, Mr. Holmes, except for one small detail. It really did exist. Just as the Island of Atlantis actually existed and was destroyed, the City of Mu also existed and was destroyed. The pointed difference between Atlantis and Mu is that the one goal of the populace of Mu was world domination. They too, were technologically brilliant with advanced science, but they were entirely evil. When their island city was destroyed, we Atlanteans believed there were no survivors; that their threat to the world was over. Apparently, some did survive, and they have remained hidden until now."

Chapter 9. Another Most Unusual Turn of Events, (Who would have imagined yet another lost civilization?)

Captain Nemo sighed and continued, "The Atlanteans let the knowledge of the Lost City of Mu slip into myth, fable, and disbelief, so that it might be forgotten, and the dark influence of Mu would be removed from the world. But it seems a small group of them have survived over the eons, and their goals have not changed. They still seek world domination.

Luna acquiesced and agreed. "It is true. They slip in and out of the shadows collecting scientific information and knowledge that will help them recreate their reign of terror. I first came across them when they were creating the underwater structure we have just encountered. Being unaware of their past, I initially believed that they were scientists seeking to learn the secrets of the ocean first hand, by living underwater where they could observe the beauty of the sea and experience all the ocean offers. One member of their organization even seemed friendly at first, but later I realized their true nature, which is cruel and evil. They have no regard for life, human or otherwise.

"They believe that Monsieur Verne has knowledge of the future, as well as, time travel, and that they can extract that information from him to their benefit. That is why I chose to reveal my existence to you to aid in freeing him from their grasp. He is a good and kind man. He and I have had many conversations during the time he was voyaging on his yacht...."

Before Luna could continue, a crew member returned to the air lock chamber and informed us that two of the sperm whale submersibles had been sighted following us at a distance, and these two whales appeared to be somewhat larger than the one we had previously encountered.

Captain Nemo turned to her and said, "Luna, you have a greater familiarity with this group and their submersibles. Do those craft contain any offensive weapons that could be used against the *Nautilus*?"

She nodded affirmatively and replied, "They each carry two cylindrical explosive devices that can be launched towards other vessels. I have seen them do so. They have used them to sink unsuspecting ships. The explosions are small but powerful. The projectiles are not very fast though, and if they miss their target, they just continue on in the direction they are launched until they lose momentum and fall to the ocean floor. They only seem to explode when the forward end of the projectile strikes a solid surface."

Sherlock, who had been staring off into the distance while Luna spoke, suddenly interjected. "Captain, unless Jules Verne's novel left out some details on offensive weapons aboard the *Nautilus*, I deduce that you only have the ramming spur and the electrical charge to the hull: is that correct?" The Captain shook his head affirmatively, and Sherlock continued, "Luna, can you tell me the distance from which they can effectively fire their weapon? And do you know of any unexploded projectiles-- I believe they are called torpedoes-- that may have come to rest on the ocean floor in our current vicinity? I have a plan that will stop the two pursuing craft."

Luna thought for just a moment before answering. "I would say that the effective distance of their weapon is only five times the length of the *Nautilus*. Regarding any unexploded torpedoes, Captain can you show me on the chart where we are now. I have seen several of them near the area we just left."

Captain Nemo pointed out on the chart the seamount where we had started from and where we currently were at the moment. Luna examined the chart briefly and pointed out a position. "There! There are two of them resting on a rise right in this area here. I am sure I could locate them again. What did you have in mind, Mr. Holmes?"

"Well as I see it, the torpedo hitting a solid surface should be no different than a solid surface impacting the front of the torpedo. We lead their submersibles in a wide circle that takes them back over their torpedoes sitting on the ocean floor and

83

then detonate them from a distance. That should immobilize the two vessels."

"And how do you propose that we detonate them?" asked Captain Nemo.

"Just after we pass over the devices, we drop two divers with your underwater rifles at a safe enough distance from the intended explosion. The impact of the rifle projectile on the front of the torpedo should be sufficient to set it off. The question is, what is the range of your underwater rifle, and is it far enough to set off the explosion without harm to the divers?"

Captain Nemo thoughtfully replied, "I designed and built those rifles. I am an expert in their use, and I would stake my life on my ability to hit those torpedoes from a safe distance, but I don't believe that any of my crew would be accurate enough at that interval. Your plan is sound, but will it require my skill to be able to hit the exact point that will set off those torpedoes. I will only be able to fire at and detonate one of them."

"Not necessarily," added Sherlock. "There is another way to detonate the torpedo. Luna, if she is agreeable to this plan, can place a metal bowl attached to long enough lines over the curved front of the second torpedo, and when the whale submersibles are directly over them, we provide a strong enough force to pull the bowl against the front of the torpedo, and that will provide the necessary impact to set off the explosive. All you need to do is put holes near the rim of a solid metal bowl and attach lines to it. She can lead the lines back to a safe place from where your divers can provide the brute force."

While it was an interesting approach, and it could work, I was concerned for her safety and expressed my thoughts. "Luna that would be a dangerous task and you could get injured."

She looked at me with a surprised expression and responded. "I thank you for your concern, Dr. Watson. That is very kind of you, but I have lived my entire life underwater in an environment full of predators, dangers, and worse. I have even survived several marriage proposals from overly amorous sailors. If Captain Nemo's crew can create the device, then I can safely place it in position."

The Captain gave his crew orders to prepare the items we would need and to adjust the course to allow us to slowly circle back to the position which Luna had indicated. We monitored the position of the two whale submersibles as we made ready everything we needed. The captain and two of his crew donned their underwater breathing suits and equipment, and Luna carefully gathered the bowl and lines. To my surprise, she handed them to me to hold on to while she stated that she had to go swim ahead to find the exact location of the torpedoes, and that she would be back to take the detonation device from me after she had located them and set the *Nautilus* on the right track. She cautioned me to be careful and that as soon as she retrieved the bowl and lines, to drop the two divers that would provide the pulling force. Then when we had passed them to a safe distance, Captain Nemo would exit to his position forward of the torpedoes.

I must say that Sherlock had come up with some clever and complicated plans in the past, but this was by far the most unusual. Luna smiled at me and dove into the pool of water in the air chamber room while the crew, stationed at the viewing ports, reported on her progress as well as the status of the two craft that were pursuing us. I waited and wondered if she would locate the devices where she expected them to be and if they would be oriented correctly and if they were even still functional. What if the plan failed? Would I ever see her again? There was so much I wanted to ask her. It all seemed so strange, yet I felt somehow connected to her.

My thoughts were broken by a crew member exclaiming, "She has found the torpedoes and indicated our course. Be ready to hand off the detonator." My hands were trembling as I stood ready and waiting for her to reappear. Just as she broke the surface of the water in the entry pool, I thrust the device into her hands and almost fell in after her. I fortunately recovered my balance so the two divers were able to depart. Just as they did, one of the other crew members announced, "Captain, it looks like the whale submersibles are preparing to fire their weapons. The forward mouth section of the whales has opened."

Captain Nemo resolutely answered, "We must go through with this!" and he exited with his underwater rifle, as we had reached the point where he could safely fire from. I could see nothing from where I was, but the crew at the aft facing viewing ports stated that it appeared that everything was in position and we just had to wait until the Mu craft were over the torpedoes, and hope they did not fire at us before then. Sherlock instructed the crew to be ready to drop all ballast immediately if the whale craft did fire, which was fortunate, for the first submersible launched a torpedo at us just as it passed over our trap.

"Torpedo launched!" Cried one of the crew. "Drop all ballast!" Then I heard two distant explosions over the rush of water being released from the *Nautilus* and felt the turbulence of the two torpedoes detonating while the *Nautilus* quickly ascended out of the path of the weapon that had been fired at us. As the turbulent water and silt cleared, the crew reported Sherlock's plan had worked perfectly, as both craft were disabled, and he could see Captain Nemo waving to indicate that he was unharmed.

"What about Luna?" I asked. "Do you see her anywhere? Is she okay? And how did your divers fare?"

As we were safe from the torpedo that had been fired at us and missed, the helmsman reduced the speed of the *Nautilus*, and turned back to retrieve Captain Nemo, Luna, and the two divers. The crew at the portholes reported both submersibles had released their water ballast and ascended to the surface where they were apparently powerless. The *Nautilus* crew contacted their fellow crewmen on board Verne's yacht to let them know of the two disabled vessels, as we would need to continue on our course after we had everyone back on board. We first picked up Captain Nemo, who, as soon as he had removed his breathing helmet, congratulated Sherlock on his plan. Sherlock responded by complimenting the Captain on his marksmanship. The captain replied, "I was able to detonate the one torpedo, but it was your makeshift device that set off the second one. What do we know of Luna and my divers?"

"We are coming up to our divers now," a crew member replied. "But there is no sign of the mermaid."

I worriedly wondered what could have happened to her. She must have reached a point of safety with the lines, if the divers were able to detonate the second torpedo. Perhaps they could provide some information when they came aboard.

Chapter 10. A Most Unusual Dilemma,
(And a new plan of action.)

As soon as the crewmen, who had been assigned the task of pulling the detonation lines, reentered the air lock chamber and removed their breathing equipment, Captain Nemo questioned them as to what had happened and if they had seen Luna anywhere.

"We saw her swim towards the torpedo with the bowl device, but she never brought the lines back to us. We don't know if she detonated the device or if the explosion from the torpedo that you fired at caused it to explode, but it was not us. We did not see any trace of her after the turbulence and sediment cleared. Should we go back out and search for her?"

I was about to say yes, of course, they must go back and look for her, but the Captain replied, "This is a most unusual and difficult dilemma. Every second we wait, could put Jules Verne's life in greater danger and give the enemy an advantage, if they gain any information from him. We have already lost considerable time in stopping the two vessels that were pursuing us. We cannot lose any more time."

"We would not even be here if she had not gone out there to stop them!" I exclaimed. "How can you think of going on without her?" In my mind I saw her injured and left behind, helpless. I longed to have told her my feelings for her before she had departed.

Captain Nemo solemnly replied, "I appreciate your concern, Dr. Watson, I was out there as well, we both understood the risks. This is not an easy decision. What is your opinion, Mr. Holmes?"

Sherlock looked from me to the Captain and answered, "It should be quite obvious. If you did not see her anywhere in front of the torpedoes up to where you were stationed and your divers did not see her anywhere behind the torpedoes up to the location where they were waiting, then for some reason, she swam either to the left or to the right. My conclusion is that one of the torpedoes had somehow been shifted in its orientation to our course on the sea floor, and she could not lead the lines back to where the divers were waiting. She had to lead the lines sideways, or the plan would not have worked. There was always a fifty percent possibility of that happening. I am quite sure she is out there and will be along any moment."

I was staring intently into the entry pool, wondering where she could be, wishing she would return, and very concerned for her safety, when much to my surprise and relief, the surface of the water in the entry pool burst forth as Luna suddenly emerged from the water, completely drenching me for the second time that day. She once again, sat on the edge of the pool with a playful smile as she commented, "My dear Dr. Watson, you are completely soaked. You will catch a terrible cold if you are not careful. You do understand that I did not do that on 'porpoise'. I can make you some wonderful seaweed tea. It would be quite good for you." Then looking at the Captain, she inquired, "What are we still doing here? The pursuing craft have been neutralized. We should be heading to that island as quickly as possible."

As the captain gave the command to resume the previous heading at full speed, I answered her. "We were concerned about you! I was concerned about you. You never brought the lines back to the divers, and they did not see you after the explosions. What happened?"

Her answer echoed Sherlock's deduction to a T. "The second torpedo had changed position 90 degrees, and the divers were not in the correct location to provide the proper pulling force. I had to lead the lines off to the left to make the detonation device properly function. You know there was always a fifty percent probability of that happening. Fortunately, I have the strength of a dolphin when I need it. It has come in quite handy on many occasions."

I did not know what to say. She sounded just as logical as Sherlock but was entirely more attractive and most delightful to gaze upon. I must confess, in spite of being completely soaked in sea water again, I could not take my eyes away from her. I was so pleased that she had not been injured or worse. And did she call me "dear"? As we continued on our course, she asked what our plan was when we arrived at their base.

Sherlock took the lead and answered, "Well, that would again depend on what we find. You say they have an airship of some type. That gives them a certain advantage. It also depends on if Jules Verne is still there. So far we have found evidence of his presence in each location that we have been to, but he has not been there. Yet, in each situation, he managed to leave a hidden clue to help us follow him. That last structure was no different."

"But Holmes!" I interrupted, "We never went into the underwater base. You just looked inside what was left of the entry hatch for only a moment or two, and then we returned to the *Nautilus*. How could you have found anything in that short time?"

Sherlock smiled with that look of his when he knows something that he and he alone is aware of. In times like those, he is the master of suspense. Just when we could wait no longer, he explained, "I knew that Jules Verne would leave us another clue, just as I knew that his captors would be careless regarding him, since they were rigging the entryway with explosives. They did not believe that anyone would get in there alive, so they paid no attention to what Verne was doing before they removed him from the facility. Knowing that there were traps, he had to leave his clue somewhere near the entrance, yet safe from the effect of the explosives. I only needed a second to retrieve this."

He held up a small watertight metal box that had the image of a mermaid engraved on its cover.

Luna cried out, "I know that box! I recovered it from a shipwreck and gave it to Monsieur Verne several years ago! It was for his birthday as a thank you for all the pleasant talks we had. He was like a father to me in explaining the ways of the surface world. I wanted him to have something to remember me by after he sold his yacht and would no longer be sailing."

I must confess that when I heard Luna refer to Jules Verne as a father figure, I was so very relieved, as my feelings for her were growing quite strong. I imagined her giving me some small token of affection. I would treasure it always.

But what could I possibly offer to her, a mermaid? I pictured us together in a moonlit sea, whispering to each other. Perhaps I could write her poem..."

Sherlock interrupted my thoughts as he continued, "And he knew that we would recognize this box as another clue from him. Let us open it and see what he has to say."

Sherlock opened the mermaid box and removed a folded sheet of paper. Carefully unfolding it, he commented, "This time it is not in any type of code. He must have had little time to write. Here is what he says: *'Being taken to island base off coast of Iceland. They seek my method of time travel to gain weapons of the future. They cannot know this, even if it costs my life. Base must be destroyed. Volcano is their power source. Use it against them. Make it erupt!'*"

Luna's eyes grew wide with concern as she responded, "The location they are going to is a volcanic island. If the volcano were to erupt, that would certainly destroy their base, but we must save him first." With a questioning look, she added, "Is it even possible for humans to cause a volcano to erupt?"

Captain Nemo cleared his throat and interjected, "It is not as difficult as one might imagine. The catastrophic explosion of Krakatau several years ago was caused by the last decedents of Lemuria when they tried to harness the energy of that volcano. They were working in hidden caverns beneath the mountain, and they lost control of their experiment. The results were devastating. That eruption claimed 36,000 lives and altered the world climate for years."

Sherlock nodded and added, "The Dutch authorities reported 36,417 to be exact, but some experts put the number at 120,000 lives lost, and the explosion was heard over 3,000 miles away. I do not think Jules Verne is suggesting anything at all of that magnitude. If we can just initiate something more localized, it could disable their communication and transportation systems as well as their weapons and construction facilities. That would trap them on their island until the proper authorities could be notified and sent to apprehend them. If this island location is their main base, then that should capture the majority of the group. They have already abandoned the underwater base that we just left. Their two large submersibles are disabled and under the control of your crew on Verne's former yacht. Luna, do you know if they have any other bases located anywhere else?"

Luna stared in the distance before replying. "I have heard mention of only one other place they sometimes travel to. It is another small volcanic island in the Atlantic Ocean, far off the coast of Portugal."

Captain Nemo replied. "That will be near the Azores. It must be a very small and well hidden facility, or our Atlantean network would have surely known about it."

Holmes responded retrospectively, "That may not be true if you are not looking for it. You and the *Nautilus* have managed to remain hidden from civilization all these years, not counting a few sea monster sightings. You stated earlier you thought all the inhabitants of Mu had perished. You have not been looking for them, so therefore, you have not seen them. We must continue to their island base near Iceland and rescue Jules Verne as well disable their main facility. Then we can investigate their final base in the Azores to finish this once and for all.

Chapter 11. Another Most Unusual Journey,
(And a very quick one at that.)

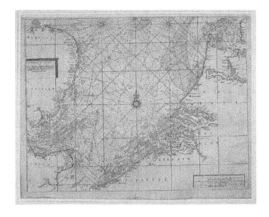

The top speed of the *Nautilus*, as described by Jules Verne in his novel, was 50 knots or nautical miles per hour. Captain Nemo confirmed Verne's claim and proudly stated there was no faster vessel above or below the surface of the ocean. We would easily reach their island base in less than ten hours. What type of power source could maintain that kind of speed was beyond my comprehension, but Sherlock seemed to have a solid grasp on the subject. He asked if Captain Nemo had read his paper entitled "*A Speculation on Hypothetical Power Sources and the Speeds Capable of Being Attained in Their Utilization*". The Captain replied that he had indeed read Sherlock's paper and, while it was interesting and creative, it had only touched the surface of a fascinating subject. If Sherlock was interested, the Captain could show him the propulsion room, to which Holmes readily agreed.

The crew had already returned to their duties, so when Sherlock and Captain Nemo left the air lock chamber, both of them deep in conversation regarding the power source of the *Nautilus*, I was at last left alone with Luna. Of course, I was still dripping wet, shivering, and at a complete loss at what to say to the most attractive female I had ever laid eyes upon, even if she did happen to be a half human, half fish, mythical creature that may have been four times older than I and at times looked just like a dolphin. What does one say in that kind of situation? "Hello. Do you know that you are the most beautiful creature in the world? What are your plans for dinner next week?"

I could not believe I had just said that! What was I thinking? I felt ridiculous, but Luna just smiled and laughed in an enchanting, melodious voice that was like crystals in the wind.

"And just what did you have in mind, my dear Dr. Watson? Afternoon tea, with scones and jam and maybe some pickled herring sandwiches, perhaps?"

I clumsily replied, "Please do call me John. Yes, afternoon tea would be lovely. That is, as long as the tea is not seaweed based."

What was I thinking??? In all the strange and unusual circumstances I had ever experienced while accompanying Sherlock, I had never found myself at such a complete loss of composure. Her eyes twinkled as she again laughed. "My dear, sweet John. You are so humorous. I do understand that seaweed tea does take some getting used to. You needn't worry about that. But I do wonder where we would go for tea. The sandwiches could get rather soggy you know."

To emphasize her point as she replied, with a grand flourish, she swirled her tail and again doused me with sea water from the pool. I slowly came to my senses about the shear impossibility of the situation as she gently took my hand and stated, "You are very sweet and a true gentleman, but you are also soaking wet, shivering, and you need to get into dry clothes before you do catch cold. Do not worry, John Watson. I will not disappear. We have a task to complete in rescuing Monsieur Verne."

Still in a bit of a daze, I agreed and left the air lock chamber to go back to the cabin that was mine and change into dry clothes. When I arrived there, I discovered my own clothes had been dried and were left folded on the table. It felt good to be back in my original attire. I somehow felt more grounded in reality. I was myself again and not some love struck school boy. Yet still, I could not shake my thoughts and feelings about Luna. I knew the sheer impossibility of the situation, but it did not stop me from wondering. To help me sort things out, I tried putting my thoughts down on paper but only ended up writing a poem to Luna. I had to face the fact. I was head over heels drowning in my feelings for her, and logical or not, she was a mermaid. She was not only ravishing, but intelligent and charming as well. But I was, quite exhausted from the previous day's adventure that had led right into this journey without a moment's rest, and I soon found myself sound asleep and dreaming that I was drowning. I dreamt the ocean was swallowing me and I could not breathe! I was helplessly being pulled out to sea as Luna sat on rock singing and calling to me like a mythical siren. I was about to go under for the last time, when thank goodness, Sherlock showed up at my door to wake me. Leave it to Sherlock Holmes to provide a life preserver in the form of his cold logic regarding our task of rescuing Jules Verne. Not to mention stopping the organization that had kidnapped him.

"Watson, you need to get a grip on yourself," he flatly stated as he walked into the cabin with a large book in his hand. "We will need everyone focused when we reach their island base. We have to rescue Mr. Verne, disable the entire facility, and prevent anyone from escaping in their air ship. It is rather straight forward actually, but it will require your participation and full attention."

"Straight forward?" I questioned. "Just what did you have in mind? It does not sound very straight forward to me. You have never even seen the base. You have no idea what we will find there, and yet you make it sound overwhelmingly simple."

With a loud thump, Sherlock placed the large book that he had brought with him on the table and opened it to a page with a detailed map and stated, "Yes, quite simple. Good fortune is with us, Watson. It turned out, that when Luna gave us the coordinates of the island base, something about them sounded vaguely familiar to Captain Nemo. He returned to his library and searched until he found this; a set of detailed charts and maps of the caverns of this island. It appears that Captain Nemo and his crew had scouted out the entire island some time ago to determine its feasibility as a possible supply base. They are always looking for well hidden locations to use as safe havens. They determined the volcano has made the island too unstable to safely use. Apparently, the descendants of Mu thought otherwise, and according to Verne's message, they have developed some way of tapping into the magma of the volcano to power their base. If you look here, you see there is a direct path into a hidden lagoon that is close to the magma chamber. All we have to do is place a timed charge near the magma, set to go off after we exit, and it should cause a small enough eruption to disable the entire facility."

"And how do we prevent an explosive charge from going off after we place it next to pool of magma that is who knows how hot?" I asked.

Sherlock stared at the ceiling of the room as he casually replied, "Actually volcanic magma ranges between 1,300 and 2,400 degrees Fahrenheit. Considering the air temperature of Iceland this time of year, I estimate the magma will be 1,973 degrees Fahrenheit. I wrote a paper once on *"Calculating the Distance to Heat Sources at Which Explosives Will Detonate Based on Temperature of Heat Source and Quantity and Type of Explosives"*. I never thought I would have the opportunity to perform a field trial on my calculations. It should be quite informative. I hope I will have the opportunity to take notes. We will place the charge in a sealed metal box with sea ice in the box to keep it cool enough to prevent it from detonating prematurely."

"And what about the airship? How will we prevent it from taking off and escaping?" I queried.

With a dismissive wave, Sherlock explained, "That is the easiest part. At this time of year, there are significant amounts of sea ice on the surface of the ocean near the island. Using the electrical charge of *Nautilus*'s hull, we will rapidly melt a sufficient quantity of ice into the water to create a massive fog bank that will blanket the whole island. Using the fog as a cover, we can get someone close enough to the airship to disable it with a small charge.

"But Sherlock!" I exclaimed. "If the island is covered with fog, how would anyone be able to find their way to the airship or know where to place a charge to prevent it from flying? None of us have ever seen it before. And they are sure to have guards on board. Somehow their crew would need to be neutralized to be able to get near enough with the explosives. You will need someone with first hand skill in that kind of operation. It is much like some of our previous exploits."

Sherlock grabbed my hand and shook it, responding, "Good point, Watson. I am so glad that I spoke with you. Thank you for volunteering for the task. Now how do you propose to do that? Luna has seen the craft, and she can tell you how it functions, so you can determine its weak points. You will not have a great deal of time once we put our plan in motion."

I looked at him with disbelief. "How did I get shanghaied into disabling the airship?" I asked. "Sherlock, that is more underhanded than drugging sailors to get them aboard a ship."

Sherlock gave a sly look and quickly replied, "Why Watson, that is brilliant! What a clever idea! It is exactly like drugging sailors to get them aboard a ship, except you will be drugging them to keep them from getting off the ship. The *Nautilus* crew can make a very effective knockout gas out of a concentrated form of that seaweed tea. All you will have to do is get it aboard the airship to neutralize the guards so you can plant the small explosives to disable the ship. As I stated, Luna can help you determine the best approach, since she has seen it before. I am sure you won't mind talking to her again. I have seen the way you look at her."

I started to object, when he interrupted me with a wave of his hand. "Watson, don't even try to object, or explain your way out of it. I could tell your feelings for her if I was blindfolded, sound asleep, in another room, in a completely different building."

I looked at Sherlock a bit embarrassed and asked, "Is it that obvious?"

He looked at me, disdainfully, and replied, "Yes, absolutely! Even if I were in another country it would be obvious. And Watson, I do understand your situation. I still have the song of Pixy Music from our previous adventure floating about my head. I have not been able to shake it. That music has been positively haunting me since we returned from our adventure in Wonderland, so I do know what you are feeling now to some extent. Just abide to stay focused."

I nodded my head and left the cabin to learn what I could from Luna about the airship. As I walked back to the air lock chamber, it dawned on me that Sherlock had not gone into detail on how we would locate and free Jules Verne. I wondered what he had in mind. Captain Nemo and his crew had been there previously, but, it was before the descendants of Mu had adapted it as their base. Who knew what modifications had been made there? Of course, I was certain that Sherlock had a plan in mind. Sherlock always has a plan.

Chapter 12. A Most Unusual Plan,
(As well as a good deal of ice.)

I returned to the air lock chamber to find Luna inside the entrance pool resting her arms on the edge of it, while her silky black hair floated upon the azure blue water. There was no question about it. Just to gaze upon her, was complete surrender. She was astonishingly enthralling and I felt myself loosing grip and drifting out to sea never to return. Her warm embrace was all I could think of, but I reminded myself, I was there to discuss how to disable the crew of their airship. I composed myself and approached her.

"Hello Luna, it is wonderful to see you again. Sherlock tells me that you are familiar with the airship on the island. I need to determine a way to disable its crew with the use of a knockout gas that Captain Nemo's crew is preparing and then place a small explosive charge to prevent it from flying.

What can you tell me about the airship and any entry or access points?"

She turned and smiled when she saw me and replied, "Hello John Watson. You are dry once more. I can take care of that if you would like." Then as playful as a dolphin, she laughed and gave only a slight swish of her tail, which fortunately did not get me wet. But out of instinct, I backed away from the splashing water, to which she added, "What's wrong? You don't want to get wet again? If you plan to spend any time at all with me, you will have to get used to that, you know. Or would you prefer I toss some fish at you? It was so humorous to watch you try and dodge the fish on Jules Verne's yacht. You are so sweet and funny." She then gave a powerful flip of her tail and emerged fully from the pool, to sit on the edge of it.

"Yes, I have seen their airship," she stated, "It is quite similar to the one Jules Verne described in his novel *Robar the Conqueror* except it is smaller. It does have propellers on both ends and a great many that face upwards. The hull structure is similar to Monsieur Verne's former yacht, but not nearly as grand. There are large hatches on deck and several opening ports along the sides of the hull. There are no funnels that I have seen, so I do not know what powers the propellers. If you intend to disable the crew, then you will need to get the substance into the interior where the humans will be."

I thought for a moment and conjectured, "That would involve going through the deck hatches or the hull ports. Are they typically closed and secured or are they open?"

She considered my question and said, "That depends. The deck hatches are closed when they are flying but usually open when they are on the ground. I have seen long cables lead from points on the large moveable platform on the base, to something inside those hatches. It seems as if they connect them every time the airship is on the platform. The hull ports may be for weapons, because I have never seen them fully closed or secured. They are not far from ground level when airship has landed."

"That is it!" I replied. "I can drop the knockout gas canisters in through the hull ports. If Sherlock's plan to create a fog bank works, I should be able to get close enough to do that without being seen. From what you have described, I will need to damage several of the vertical lift propellers to prevent it from taking off. Do you remember how many of those there are?"

She raised her eyebrows as she concentrated a moment before answering. "There are two rows of them, perhaps five or more in each row. I have only seen the craft twice, and from the surface level of the ocean. The platform they landed on was raised above the water's surface each time it was there." Then, as if the thought had just occurred to her, she changed the subject and asked, "Do you know how they plan to locate and rescue Monsieur Verne?"

I shook my head negatively. "Sherlock did not mention that part to me, but I am sure he has something worked out. He is extremely skilled in that sort of thing. You would be impressed at all that he has accomplished."

Luna smiled softly and responded, "I see you think very highly of him. It is understandable. He is most logical. That is why the echoes of the Pixy Music he heard previously, are so troubling to him. It is because that music is so illogical. But you need not worry, he will come to understand it."

I was taken aback. "But how could you know about Pixy Music? That episode occurred when we were in Wonderland. You were here in the ocean, nowhere near where it happened. How is it possible?"

To my dismay, I did not receive an answer, as we were interrupted by Captain Nemo entering the airlock chamber.

"There you are," stated Nemo. "It is imperative we go over the timing of this plan. When we arrive at the island, you will have less than 10 minutes to disable their airship, while I place the explosive charge near the magma, and Sherlock frees Jules Verne. My crew has prepared your small explosive charges as well as your knockout gas canisters. In examining the maps of the island from our previous visit, we have determined there is only one location their airship can safely land. You will exit the *Nautilus* off shore from that point. Luna will guide you to the beach and then back to the point where we will recover you both."

I looked at Luna with an expression of surprise, and she smiled and stated, "Why John, surely you know that mermaids have a perfect sense of direction. It is like an internal compass. If I have been in a place once, I can find my way back to it with my eyes closed, swimming through a cloud of octopus ink. It is part of my nature."

We continued to converse as we went over the details of the plan. Then, as we drew near the island, the *Nautilus* began to use the hull's electrical charge on large amounts of sea ice to create the fog bank. In truth, I had found myself wondering if that part of Sherlock's plan would really work, since our success in this whole endeavor depended on using the shroud of fog as a cover to hide our movements. I needn't have worried, though, for just as Sherlock had said it would, the massive cloud of fog welled up out of the sea like a murky, nebulous monster that swallowed the entire island. Soon it would be time for us to exit the *Nautilus* and find Jules Verne.

Chapter 13. A Most Unusual Sequence of Events,
(And a glowing success.)

Sherlock's idea had worked brilliantly. A heavy, dripping, grey mist covered everything in sight. The fog was denser than anything I had ever encountered in London. It was perfect. It was almost too perfect. How was I supposed to see Luna to follow her? And how would I find the airship once we had landed? We had reached the point where I departed the *Nautilus* in a small launch that was rowed by four of Nemo's crew. Luna swam in front of us, pointing to the right or left as required. I strained to see her through the misty grey mantel that hung over the sea and repeated her directions to the oarsmen through hand signals. The oars and oarlocks had been covered with cloth to prevent them from making any noise, and the fog seemed to absorb what few sounds we did make. So far everything was going according to Holmes' plan.

We reached the shore safely, and as I stepped into the shallow water near the beach, Luna gave me the compass direction to follow, embraced me, and whispered to me, "Please do be careful." She had instinctively known unerringly where we were on the beach in relation to the map we had studied. She also knew the direction to where Captain Nemo had calculated the airship would be located. He had given me the distance in paces to where it should be anchored, so with my compass in one hand and the first of my tranquilizer canisters in the other, I stepped forward into a dense, grey blanket of icy fog that surrounded me completely. I was stepping into oblivion.

I counted to myself the paces towards my destination. *'One, two, three.'* I could not see anything. I was relying completely on the compass and the calculations. I could only hope they were correct. *'Four, five six.'* I almost stumbled on a loose rock. I stopped to listen if anyone had heard the noise, but all was still quiet. *'Seven, eight, nine, ten.'* I was half way to where it should be, and I still could not see beyond my out stretched hand. *Eleven, twelve, thirteen.'* Wait, what was that? There were voices somewhere ahead. I could not understand them or be certain where they were coming from. I proceeded more cautiously. *'Fourteen..., fifteen...'* Now I heard them again, but to the left. *'Sixteen..., seventeen...'* There it was again. Would I be discovered? If so, what would I do? I found the answer to that more quickly than I would have liked, as a guard suddenly appeared out of the fog directly before me. He was clearly more surprised than I and before he could make a sound, I instinctively knocked him unconscious with a swift right hook to the jaw. The unfortunate thing, however, is that was the hand in which I had held my compass. I had silenced the guard but destroyed my only method of navigation and determining direction. If I somehow managed to survive this, how was I to return to the beach? How would I get back to the *Nautilus*?

I was only three paces from where the airship was calculated to be, so I counted out the last steps hoping that it would be there and that I was still going in the right direction. '*Eighteen...*, *nineteen..., twent...* I abruptly came to a halt mid-count as a large dark shape loomed out of the heavy grey mist right in front of me. It was definitely where the Captain had said I would find it. I decided to worry about the return trip after I had disabled the airship and proceeded to work my way along the hull looking for the gun ports. I had only taken four steps to the right when I came across the first one. I quickly activated the first tranquilizer canister and dropped it in the port and moved on. After another eight steps I discovered the second port and repeated my action with the next canister. I again followed the hull, but it started to taper inward, so I retraced my steps in the opposite direction. I had passed both of the gun ports I had already taken care of and located the next one. I could hear a commotion inside, as the crew was reacting to the tranquilizer gas. I heard the sounds of yelling, coughing, and guards falling to the floor as they lost consciousness and collapsed. "Have a cup of seaweed tea!" I said to myself, as I thrust the next canister into the open port. I worked my way down the hull, dropping a tranquilizer canister in each port, until I had used the last one.

Captain Nemo had said that the gas would be immediately effective on the crew but would dissipate very quickly. I was to wait four minutes from the time I set off the last canister, before I ventured on board the ship to place the charges. While I was working my way down the hull, I had found what had appeared to be an entry hatch, so I retraced my steps back to it as I anxiously waited for the air to clear. After what seemed like an eternity, I was able to enter the craft to work my way up to the propeller deck. I stepped inside and saw several of the ship's crew lying unconscious. The seaweed based gas had been most effective.

I found a staircase that led to the upper deck and worked my up to the forest of masts which supported the horizontal propellers providing the lift to the airship. Shivering from the cold fog that enveloped me and a nervous perspiration that I am sure comes with handling explosives, I began to activate and place the charges on the masts. Luna had said that they were in two rows, so once I had found the first mast I was able to work my way down the row to find additional masts and place the explosives. I had finished one row without incident, when suddenly, a crewman wearing a breathing apparatus similar to the one Sherlock had used to escape the whale submersible, came blundering towards me with a small ax. The visibility was next to naught, and his vision was also restricted by the underwater gear, so I had a distinct advantage. He was swinging wildly as he came at me, but I was able to duck behind a mast to avoid him. As he passed, I pushed him toward an open hatch which he fell into with a loud crash followed by silence. That took care of him.

I finished my task, and somehow was able to work my way out through the exit without tripping over anything. The charges were all placed. All I had to do now was find a way to return to the beach without the aid of a compass. But how was I supposed to accomplish this? I decided anywhere else was better than standing next to the airship, as quite soon the explosives attached to the propeller masts would start detonating and I could get injured by flying debris. So with a deep breath, I took several steps away and immediately could not see anything. Even the vessel had been swallowed up by the dismal grey darkness. I looked all around me wondering, which direction should I head? I was lost! I didn't know what to do next, when I happened to notice a glowing spot in the sand. What could it be?

I moved towards it and immediately noticed another spot slightly further away and then another and yet another, all of them leading me in what seemed like the direction I needed to go to get back to the shore. How fortunate was that? I followed the glowing marks until I reached the land's end and saw Luna next to the launch, waving at me from the water. Somehow, her hands seemed to be glowing in the same fashion as the marks I had been following. As I sloshed through the shallow water to climb into the small vessel, she embraced me and exclaimed, "I knew the phosphorescent trail would lead you back to me." She then removed a device that had been somehow placed on the back of my belt, and explained, "That is why I attached this to your belt when I embraced you before you left. It released drops of glowing marine algae as you walked towards the airship, to help you find your way back. Hurry! We must move quickly. We have no time left."

As she had spoke, the first explosive charges on the airship's propeller masts started detonating. We departed as quickly as possible. With Luna leading us and the oarsmen rowing double speed, we made our way back to the rendezvous location where we would meet the *Nautilus*. It was only then I realized, against all odds, stumbling about in the sheer darkness of the fog bank, without a compass, I had actually succeeded. The airship was disabled, and I was somehow still alive. I only hoped that Sherlock and the Captain had been equally as successful and would be waiting for us when we returned.

Chapter 14. A Most Unusual Volcanic Eruption, (And a very pleasant reunion.)

Luna had stopped swimming and held up her hand to indicate we had arrived at the proper place when there was a great disturbance in the water from air bubbles ascending to the surface, followed by the topsides of the *Nautilus* rising out of the sea. I uttered a huge sigh of relief. They were here! Or at least the *Nautilus* was. I was certain they would not have left without Sherlock or Jules Verne. I looked forward to seeing them. Luna dove underwater to reenter the vessel via the airlock, I climbed aboard the deck, and the crewmen secured the launch to its location near the stern of the vessel. I was making my way back towards the hatch when the muffled sound of a series of loud explosions came from within the volcanic peak that dominated the view, as it protruded out of the fog bank that covered the island. The explosions all seemed to be on the seaward side of the mountain. One large blast obliterated the upper portion of the volcano and started lava flowing down the mountain side into the sea of fog, and in the direction of the base. I was astonished and transfixed at the destructive force of the eruption and the river of lava that burned its way down the slope illuminating the grey haze. We had to leave the area immediately.

I started to enter the hatch, but was taken aback by the appearance in the doorway of a medium-built man with dark hair and a thin mustache. He was wearing black clothing and tall boots and looked to be one of the crew we had captured from the first submersible.

What could have happened in my absence? How did the enemy crew get on board? I was about to take action against him when to my surprise, he spoke to me with Sherlock's voice. "Welcome back, Watson. I am glad to see you have survived your little jaunt. You succeeded, I presume. We accomplished our mission as well. We rescued Jules Verne."

Hearing Holmes' voice emitting from this strange interloper stopped me in my tracks. In absolute disbelief, I stared at him. I leaned in closer, looked him straight in the eyes, and whispered, "Sherlock, is that you?"

With a smile and a snicker, he removed the fake mustache and replied, "Of course it is, Watson. Who did you think it was? If I fooled you, then it is no surprise that nobody in the base questioned me. This is how I freed Jules Verne. Please do forgive my theatrics. Come down below, and I will tell you all about it as we head to the Azores."

I was amazed; Sherlock had come up with a perfect disguise that had given him access to the enemy's base so he could free Jules Verne. But why did he choose that particular appearance, and how could he possibly have known where in the base he would find Jules Verne? As I returned to the airlock chamber, my thoughts were swimming. Surely there is nothing in the world that is impossible for Sherlock Holmes. I anxiously looked forward to hearing how he had done it.

When I arrived in the airlock chamber with Holmes at my side, Captain Nemo, Jules Verne, and Luna were already there. Seeing Jules Verne for the first time, revealed a quiet, smiling gentleman, of enigmatic appearance. He was tall and slender, with grey hair, and a graying full beard. His smile conveyed a certain sense of peace and awareness of things beyond the norm. He did not speak English, but Sherlock, Captain Nemo, and Luna spoke French. I discovered later it was Verne whom had taught Luna to speak French during their many conversations while he was cruising on his yacht. I introduced myself to Mr. Verne with Luna translating for me, and he thanked me for my efforts in disabling the airship, with Luna translating for him. "My deepest thanks and appreciation to all of you, but how did you know where, they would be holding me?"

Sherlock smiled and began speaking in English for our benefit, with Luna translating into French for Jules Verne. "Let me explain. In examining the map of the island Captain Nemo and his crew made less than a year ago, I realized that the new occupants would have specific requirements and needs for their nefarious activities. Certain sized cave rooms would be needed for specific purposes; storage, sleeping quarters, work areas, laboratories, and so forth. They could only have made a minimum of modifications in the time since the *Nautilus* was last there with most of their work going towards tapping into the volcanic magma chamber as a power source. In studying the map of all the preexisting rooms within the cave system and with my knowledge of how the criminal mind works, I determined there was only one logical, possible place a prisoner would be held. I determined I had to access that location without being discovered. "I recalled that the crewmen of the whale submersible we sank earlier all shared the same physical features of dark hair and thin mustaches, which is not surprising if they all trace back to one heritage, that of the island City of Mu. If you remember, all of them wore a specific uniform of black clothing and tall boots. Just to be certain, I had verified with Luna that many of the occupants of the underwater base she had seen shared the similar physical features and attire. This made it very easy for me to create a disguise that would allow me to blend in perfectly with them. The dark hair and fake mustache even fooled you, Watson. You should have seen your face when you heard my voice. Please forgive me for having a bit of sport with you, but I could not resist. By knowing without a doubt where Mr. Verne would be held, and being able to blend in to their populace perfectly, I had solved half the problem. The task was as good as complete.

"At that point, I only needed a way to open the cell and return Mr. Verne to the *Nautilus* without being noticed. Since a significant amount of their activity on this island involves divers, it would not be unusual to see men walking about with diving equipment or in underwater suits. I attired myself in their standard uniform of dark clothes and tall boots, courtesy of the *Nautilus'* clothing supply. I then brought with me one of their dive helmets. It was the one I had retrieved from the Mu submersible along with some dark clothes and boots for Mr. Verne. The prison cell was clearly where I had determined it to be, and I walked right up to the cell location without anyone questioning me.

"I was quietly able to render the guard outside the cell unconscious using venom derived from a cone shell specimen Captain Nemo had supplied me with from one of his aquariums. I had recalled my recent paper on *"Gastropod and Cone Shell Based Toxins, Venoms, and Tranquilizers, and Their Practical Applications"*, and quite fortunately, he had a living example of the Magician Cone Snail, *Conus Magus*, on board. Its venom is one thousand times more powerful than morphine, and the effect is near instantaneous. I was able to extract the amount I needed to make a very effective tranquilizer. After the guard was incapacitated, I had access to his cell keys, so I had no problem opening and entering it. Once inside, the diver attire and the helmet provided an acceptable disguise for Mr. Verne. He did an excellent job of looking quite casual and normal wearing the dive mask to hide his beard while we returned to the rendezvous location to meet the Captain.

"By the time I had returned with Jules Verne, Captain Nemo had placed the charges in the magma chamber, and we were able to escape in the *Nautilus*. As I told Dr. Watson earlier, it was quite straight forward. I did hear the smaller explosions, which, if I am correct, would be the blasts disabling their airship. I assume that your task, Watson, was a glowing success?"

I looked at Luna and smiled at the thought of her and replied, "Yes it was, Sherlock, literally a glowing success."

"Excellent!" voiced Captain Nemo. "And the explosive charges we placed near the magma worked perfectly to cause the volcano to erupt without blowing the island as well as ourselves completely out of existence."

"Monsieur Verne says, that is good to know," Luna translated for Jules Verne. "But he wonders how you were able to get near enough to the magma chamber. When he first arrived at their island base, their mechanism that drew power from the heat of the molten material was located directly adjacent to the magma, and there were always men nearby working with it."

"That is a good question," replied Captain Nemo. "The answer lies in our previous visit to the island. The main underwater entrance to the hidden lagoon is quite visible to any submersible craft, and that is, indeed, where they entered, and the lagoon that it leads to is where they connected their power source to the magma chamber. That would be the obvious choice for their access point."

"But there was another less obvious entrance to a cavern on the other side of the magma chamber. When we left a year ago, we made certain that the second entrance was well hidden, so if we ever needed to return, we would be able to do so unnoticed. I was able to set the charges on the magma chamber without any of the Mu descendants realizing what I had done."

"That is why the initial explosions were all on the seaward side of the peak," I remarked.

"You are correct, Dr. Watson," he replied. "The secret lagoon and hidden access are both on the seaward side. We were able to control both the direction and magnitude of the eruption. It worked very well. With their airship disabled and their last submersible destroyed in the eruption, they will be stranded on the island until European authorities can be notified to send a force to apprehend them."

Sherlock turned to Jules Verne and, speaking in French asked if he could describe anything more about the group. Verne answered with Luna translating his response. "When they kidnapped me from the *Saint-Michel III*, I did not know why or who they were. They seem to be very confident in their actions, as if they are not concerned about possible repercussions. They transported me via a small whale-shaped submersible to their underwater base, and then via the airship to this island. I must say, it was rather like being in one of my *Voyages Extraordinaire*. The technology was fascinating. I am sure I would have enjoyed it more if I were not being held prisoner. I tried to leave coded, hidden clues behind in each location, hoping the right person would find them. I know that Captain Nemo had been watching after me, and I am glad he contacted you, Mr. Holmes, when I went missing. Thank goodness for your perceptiveness and skills in observation. You were able to discover and correctly decipher each of my hidden, coded messages."

"Of course," Sherlock answered, "but Luna was most helpful in directing us and providing information."

Luna smiled and blushed somewhat as she translated Verne's response to Sherlock. "Ah, yes, Luna. I was not sure how to explain her. How does one tell an unknown benefactor, or even you, Captain Nemo who I have known for so long, that you should look to a mermaid for assistance? You would not have believed me. And I must think of Luna as well. The only way to keep her safe is to keep her existence secret. The world cannot know about her. Perhaps many years in the future her story can be fully told, but I digress. I was talking about my captors.

"The members of this group, while they all share the same background, speak several different languages, and they seem to have a main contact somewhere in Europe with whom they are working. It is someone who is providing for their financial resources. Who it is, I never discovered. I did overhear, that as soon as they have learned the secret to time travel, they intend to use it to gain access to the weapons of the future. Consequently the empire will be unstoppable.

They laughed at the word "empire". I believe they intend to betray their benefactor once they achieve their goal. I am afraid this is all I can tell you. I was kept locked away most of the time. They had planned to interrogate me in depth at their main base, which you destroyed just in time. I tried to tell them my stories are based only on extensive research of existing inventions, that I know nothing of the future, but they did not believe it. I assure you they learned nothing from me while I was in their captivity, but somehow they did already know about the existence of time travel, and their technology seemed quite advanced. How is that possible?"

Captain Nemo nodded affirmatively, and replied, "Yes, that is the question. We hope to discover that when we get a response from our communications operator regarding the doctored message you composed, Sherlock. So far nothing has been noticed, but I will let you know as soon as we discover something.

"But right now, let us celebrate our success. We have freed Jules Verne from his captors, prevented them from gaining knowledge of the future, and struck a sound blow against them by rendering their airship inoperable and stranding them on the island. Thank you, Sherlock Holmes and Dr. Watson for your invaluable assistance. And Luna, thank you for all that you have done."

Luna smiled, flourished her tail, and laughingly said, "I only did what I 'cod', even if it was a bit 'fishy' at times." At which she laughed at her word play even more.

Chapter 15. Yet, Another Most Unusual Journey,
(And Sherlock plays the violin!)

At the speed the *Nautilus* was traveling, it would take us thirty-two hours to travel to the Azores, the location of the final base of the Mu descendants. What would be waiting for us there we had no idea. The Captain had contacted his Atlantean compatriot posted in Great Britain, to inform him of the group that we had left stranded on the Icelandic island. The agent would know how to inform the proper authorities about them with a suitable reason for them to be arrested and contained.

Now it was just a matter of waiting until we arrived in the Azores. We had been working almost non-stop in locating and rescuing Jules Verne, so Captain Nemo suggested we rest a while, and he provided another magnificent seafood dinner for us with sincere apologies for the lack of marinated giant squid tentacles, but a strong recommendation for the sautéed sea cucumber. He even provided a comfortable accommodation for Luna that allowed her to be in the salon and yet still be in contact with sea water. A large container filled with salt water and a chair made it possible for her to join us, but to my dismay, she spent a good deal of time conversing in French with Jules Verne. I knew she had been very concerned about him, but I still felt somewhat disappointed.

Sherlock sat down beside me. "Feeling at a loss, Watson old boy? Don't worry, she has feelings for you. I can see that clearly, but you must realize there would be more than just a small amount of difficulty in getting serious with someone so water bound as she is. At least when this adventure is over, you will be able to go back to 221-B Baker Street and forget all about this. I wish I could do the same with the Pixy Music we heard on our prior adventure in Wonderland. I have not been able to get her melody out of my head no matter what I do. I have even considered taking some of that cone shell anesthetic that I used on the guard to help me escape from it."

I looked at him intensely and asked, "Sherlock, is it really that terrible?"

He emphatically shook his head back and forth and replied, "No, no. It is not at all bad. Don't even think that, Watson. It is the most beautiful sound I have ever heard. But I cannot escape from it. It seems it is always there, an echo in the background, calling to me from a distance. It is a captivating and enchanting melody I can't quite hear. This song! This is unlike anything I have previously experienced."

I thought for a moment before answering. "You know you are trying to approach this with logic, keeping it at a proper distance. Have you considered embracing it?"

"What are you talking about, Watson?" He replied.

"You can't seem to escape it, Sherlock. Why don't you just embrace the music? Play along with it. I am sure the Captain has a violin here somewhere. He always seems to have whatever we may happen to need tucked away in the hold of the *Nautilus*. In fact, I would not at all be surprised to learn that he has a Stradivarius on board."

Just then, Captain Nemo approached us with a violin case in his hand and addressed Sherlock. "Mr. Holmes, since we have some time before we get to the Azores, and we are celebrating, may I ask you to indulge us with some violin music? I have heard you are quite the virtuoso on the strings. I have an excellent quality Stradivarius in perfect condition here that is just longing to be played."

Holmes looked at me intensely, raised his eyes to the ceiling, inhaled deeply and let out a long breath. I shrugged my shoulders and stated I did not have a thing to do with the Captain's suggestion. Sherlock accepted the violin case from Nemo and, with great care, set it on the table and opened it. He stared at it for some time before gently removing it, and placing it at his shoulder. He picked up the bow, hesitating, almost trembling for a moment, and then began to play.

I cannot say if it was the quality of the violin or the mystical music that had been playing continuously in his head, but I had never heard Sherlock play so magnificently in all my life. The music was unlike anything he had played previously, and it is well known he himself owns a Stradivarius he acquired from a broker for a mere 55 shillings. How he managed it is anyone's guess. At last estimate, it was stated to be worth 500 guineas. At that moment, traveling through the undersea world, Sherlock's music was truly magnificent.

He did not have any sheet notes in front of him, and I must confess that what I heard closely resembled the ethereal music I recall from our previous adventure in Wonderland. I know this may sound strange, but it is almost as if he were playing a duet with the entrancing Pixy Music playing one side and Sherlock playing the other. There were clearly two exquisite and distinctive lines of music being played, each interweaving with the other, floating back and forth and creating an ethereal harmony. It was infinitely enchanting.

When Sherlock finished playing and set the violin back in its case, there was not a sound in the salon beyond the background humming of the machinery of the *Nautilus*. We sat there in silence not knowing what to say. Sherlock slowly closed the violin case, and as he walked past me to leave the salon, he leaned over and whispered so that I alone could hear him say, "She spoke to me." And he left the room.

All of us had been mesmerized by the music, but after he exited, the conversation picked up again.

Luna began by mirthfully expressing, "That was most enjoyable and also rather familiar. He is really quite the musician, isn't he?"

I nodded and replied with a smile, "Yes, but I have also heard that mermaids are very gifted in music as well."

She laughed and replied, "Do not believe everything you hear about mermaids, John Watson. After all, how many people do you know have actually seen one?"

She translated what she had said for Jules Verne, who just nodded and smiled. I replied, "Now that you mention it, I do believe I can truthfully say that everyone in this room has seen a mermaid, and a most beguiling one, at that."

Like a playful dolphin, she splashed the water in her container and responded, "You are so funny, my dear John Watson."

I would have liked to respond to her, but one of Captain Nemo's crew entered the salon with a concerned expression and handed the Captain a message. He read it with a scowl on his face and said, "If you will all excuse me, I must go find Sherlock Holmes. He needs to see this."

Chapter 16. Yet Another Most Unusual Discovery, (And I am certain Sherlock suspects something.)

We were taken aback by the abrupt change in Captain Nemo after he had read the message. What could it have been that had affected him so severely? We silently wondered and imagined, until he returned to the salon with Sherlock following closely behind him.

Holding up the message, Captain Nemo began speaking as Luna again translated into French for Jules Verne. "We have determined the location of the leak in our communication network. It is somewhere in London, England. We had been transmitting Sherlock's fabricated message to determine the source of the compromise, to only one of our agents at a time, so we can watch for an indication it has been intercepted, and as of yet, we have not seen the expected response. We had not sent the fake message to our operative in Great Britain. But it appears the genuine message I sent to our agent in the British government regarding the group of hostiles we left on the volcanic island has been intercepted. He reports that a ship has suddenly been chartered for a very "urgent" trip to a small island off the coast of Iceland. The party chartering the vessel said that price is no object. They will pay whatever the ship owner requested. Their only concern is speed. They have already left for the island."

Captain Nemo looked at us and went on. "Friends, we now know that the communication break is within the British government. It will take some time to determine a more exact location and the individuals involved. I must request that, as soon as we complete our business in the Azores, we head directly back to England to find the party responsible."

I raised a question, "Yes that makes perfect sense, but what of the group of hostiles we left stranded on the island? If their people get to the island first, then they will be set loose. That would be a major blow to us. The party that set out to free them has to be stopped. However, you cannot have your agent call for the military to sink a privately chartered vessel. The owner and his crew are innocent people who just happen to be on board. It is not done in the civilized world."

Nemo looked directly at me and replied, "I am sure that if the Mu descendants reach the island and free the group stranded there, they will kill the owner and crew of the chartered vessel, as they will have no further use for them. These people do not respect the laws of civilization, and accordingly, they do not deserve the consideration of those same laws. I do not look to the military to intervene. I will stop them. The *Nautilus* and my crew have existed outside of the awareness and laws of your society for years, so I will deal with the Mu descendants. But you need not worry, Dr. Watson. I am not going to sink the chartered vessel or harm its crew. My only intent is to damage the vessel and render it incapable of reaching Iceland so they cannot free the group we left there. The military can then rescue the ship owner and his crew, and tow them back to London as well as arrest their passengers. This will cause a slight detour and delay in our trip to the Azores, as well as some inconvenience to the ship owner, well worth the cost of saving his life and that of his crew even if he never knows it. Now if you will please excuse me, I must get an accurate description of the chartered vessel and plot an intercept course. From this point on, all communications will be double coded."

As Captain Nemo left the salon, Sherlock looked up and commented. "It is pleasing to see that my idea to send a fabricated message to determine the location of the communication breach worked, even if it was Captains Nemo's genuine message that achieved the same goal. But it is very concerning to me that the intercept location is in London, England. That makes me wonder about the exact nature and source of the compromise. I must deliberate on this."

With that, Sherlock turned to the library shelves as if we did not exist, began scanning the books, occasionally pulling one or more out and throwing them onto the table. I would have wondered about his actions, but the library held a great many reference books in addition to fictional novels. After completing his search of the book shelves, he sat down and started examining them while looking at the chart that depicted

England in the greatest detail. As far as Sherlock was concerned, we could have been in a different ocean.

I turned to Luna and asked her what she thought of the Captain's plan. She shrugged her shoulders looking quite graceful in the process, and very straightforwardly replied, "His plan is almost sound, but I think you will need to launch some more of the seaweed tea knockout gas canisters at them just to be safe. They may be rather 'crabby' when their vessel is damaged."

I looked at her with a surprised expression and was about to say something when she laughed and stated, "You did not think I was serious did you?" And then she gave a slight flourish of her tail to splash some water in my direction.

"Well of course not, Luna," I replied. "But do be cautious about splashing salt water on Captain Nemo's Persian rugs, they are quite old."

With a coy smile she responded, "But not as old as I am. I met the gentleman that wove that rug. It was completed on a Wednesday during a waxing moon. I could tell you his name, but it is 27 characters long and not easy to pronounce."

Jules Verne excused himself to return to his cabin to rest, as he had been through a great ordeal with the kidnapping and the rescue. While he was leaving, he thanked us again and gave Luna a kiss on her forehead.

We were finally alone, or somewhat alone as Sherlock was still there, but he was so engrossed in his deliberating that I could have paraded a forty-foot cephalopod, a Narwhale, which is the Unicorn of the sea, and Poseidon himself right past Sherlock, and he would never have noticed. I asked Luna what she had meant when she had said that the violin music sounded familiar. She responded with a dreamy smile as if she was remembering something pleasant from a long time ago, and answered, "The haunting ethereal songs of Pixy Music are not easily forgotten. Your friend, Sherlock Holmes, has made that realization, and is having a difficult time understanding it. They do not fit into his framework of logic and rational thinking."

"But who or what is Pixy Music?" I asked her. "The Unicorn from Wonderland appeared to be acquainted with her, and explained to us she wove a "sphere of protection" around the time machine with her music to protect us during our return trip, but she never actually appeared. None of us ever saw her. And how is it that you are aware of her. To my knowledge, she is from Wonderland, and you are from the seas here in our world."

Our conversation was loudly interrupted as Sherlock pounded a fist on the table and exclaimed, "It cannot be! It just cannot be!"

I glanced in his direction with concern and asked, "What is it Sherlock? What's wrong? Did you discover where the communication was intercepted?"

He looked up as if he had suddenly noticed we were there, and then dismissively replied, "No, no, I think I just misread something. Everything is fine. Go on with your conversation about forty-foot cephalopods, Narwhales, and Poseidon, or whatever it was you two were talking about."

We were about to continue, when Captain Nemo returned to the salon and stated, "I have the course and descriptive information on the chartered vessel. They will not be far from the track we are currently following. It should be easy to recognize their ship when we come across it. We will damage their craft just enough to make certain they cannot get to that island, and then we can return to our original course to the Azores. The fact they chartered a vessel tells me they did not have any more of their submersibles available. That is excellent news. That means we are making progress."

Looking at the profusion of books and papers scattered about the table, Captain Nemo asked Sherlock, "And what about you, Mr. Holmes? Have you made any progress on the calculations you have been working on? If you don't mind my asking, what exactly have you been working on?"

Sherlock answered that he was investigating where, specifically the communication breech in England had occurred, but so far, he had not discovered anything conclusive. His previous sudden outburst and something in the tone of his voice told me that he knew more than he had disclosed, but he had his reasons for not sharing what he had learned at that time. I did not question his reply, but I stared at him and wondered.

The Captain then turned to Luna and said, "We will soon be approaching the vessel that we will be taking action against. We must return your portable accommodation to the airlock chamber. If anything happens, you will have quicker access back to the ocean."

She looked at him and answered, "If anything happens to the *Nautilus*, it would most likely fill with sea water, which as you are well aware, I have lived in for all my life. Your logic is 'all wet'. But if you insist, I will return to the water pool chamber. How do you endeavor to disable their ship?"

Captain Nemo replied the ship in question had a pair of side paddle wheels and a stern propeller. He would first pass a safe distance under the craft and release two very small explosives attached to cork flotation devices directly under the vessel on both sides so they would be drawn up into the side paddle wheels, rendering them inoperable. Nothing too large, so as not to damage the hull, just enough to ascertain their paddle wheels are out of operation, and he would then incapacitate their main propeller with his ramming spur. That will make certain they do not get to their base near Iceland, but on the other hand will not sink them.

"But how can you be certain that the explosives will damage the paddle wheels? What if they miss their mark?" asked Sherlock. "Any number of things could cause them to go astray. I can list five possibilities, three probabilities, and one absolute certainty, without even trying. Not to mention random chance."

Luna chimed in saying, "I could attach them to the paddles. That will make sure they reach the right location. I could exit the *Nautilus* underwater and wait for them. When they pass by, I can swim up and place the charges on the paddle wheels. You could pick me up before you disable their propeller."

Sherlock answered her, "Luna, I admire your courage, and your idea has merit, but it is simply too dangerous for you to try to get that close to the vessel and the turning paddle wheels traveling at such a high speed. The vortex of the turning wheels could create a suction that could trap you near them. Might I suggest you attach your explosive charge to the cork float, using a long enough line, you can remain a safe distance away from the vessel as it goes past. Position the float in the path of the side wheel. The turning wheel will capture the float, drawing it upward, wrapping the tether around the paddle, which will bring the explosive up to the wheel box.

"It does sound like a safer approach," I said, "but how much time would Luna have to get out of the range of the blast, and is there any chance that the turning paddle wheel could dislodge the charge from the line that is attached to the cork float? If that happens, then the explosive would be falling directly down towards Luna.

Captain Nemo responded confidently, "The blast will be small and localized, just enough to destroy the paddle wheel without damaging the hull. I am sure my crew and I can construct a device that will work perfectly without any danger of breaking the tether. And it will allow enough time for Luna to safely retreat from the area. We will begin working on it immediately."

Chapter 17. A Most Unusual Revelation,
(And who would question it considering the source?)

The Captain left to begin work on his explosive device, and Sherlock was immediately again lost in his examination of the communication breach. The intensity and concerned look I saw in the expression on his face still told me that he had found something of grave consideration but did not want to reveal it just yet. Several of Nemo's crew arrived to transport Luna and her salt water chair back to the airlock chamber.

"Do be cautious with that, gentlemen," Luna teased. "You would not want to spill salt water on Captain Nemo's Persian rugs, not to mention you would not want to spill me. Who knows the storms, shipwrecks, and disasters an angry mermaid could cause? Why the great flood that wiped out all the dinosaurs would be like a summer shower compared to what I can provoke."

Luna laughed at the look of fear in the crewmen's faces and then cheerfully told them, "Do not worry. I would not let anything happen to the *Nautilus*. The seven seas are my friends. I know that because they always 'wave' at me." Then looking at their confusion she added, "Really, it is okay, it is a 'shore' thing."

Luna's playful humor and bewitching smile had me again lost in my thoughts about what would happen when this adventure was concluded. I accompanied them back to the air lock chamber, where Luna dove into the entry pool. I looked at her and saw myself someday having to say goodbye to her for the last time. I did not know what to say.

Luna, however, sloshed water at me with her tail, and said, "You look sad, John Watson. What is it that bothers you? Have you sat on a porcupine fish? That is not the 'point' of them you know."

I smiled at her playful humor, as I sat on the edge of the entry pool rim, and not wanting to tell her my true feelings yet, I answered, "I am concerned for your safety. It will be dangerous when you go out to disable that ship."

With a thrust of her tail she propelled herself out of the pool to sit on the edge next to me. "Oh dear sweet John, you are so caring. You must realize that living in the ocean, my entire life has been filled with danger. It is almost like spending one's life searching for hidden clues, solving mysteries, and chasing after dangerous villains. Can you even imagine what that must be like?"

I questioningly looked at her and with a twinkling in her eyes, and the sweetest laugh, she gave me a kiss on my cheek and dove back into the pool.

She is such a conundrum. I was completely enamored by her charm, beauty, playfulness, and intelligence, and yet I found myself at a loss for words when I was around her. Sherlock had made it clear there was no logical way the two of us could ever be together. Her existence itself is illogical, and yet there she was, right before my eyes. I sat in silence as she cavorted in the entry pool bursting with laughter as she occasionally splashed water in my direction. Finally, I recalled a question unanswered from our previous conversation. I asked her, "You never mentioned to me; how is it that you are familiar with Pixy Music from Wonderland."

With a splash, she again emerged from the pool to sit by my side and replied, "Oh, yes, I remember. We were interrupted. Something about a communication break in England causing the end of civilization as you know it. There was some truth to your comment about mermaids being gifted in music. We are very attuned and sensitive to all different types of music from all different realms. We can hear and sing across dimensions, if you understand what I mean. Pixies are mystical beings who have that same ability. They generate music that transcends distance and space for those that are attuned to it. Your friend, Sherlock

Holmes, is now very attuned to the song of Pixy Music since he heard it so clearly in your previous journey and truly embraced it moments ago when he played the violin. She will now be with him forever. From this day forth, whenever you hear Sherlock Holmes playing the violin, you are hearing him speak to Pixy Music, as she is speaking to him though her song. She will be a part of him forever, even if they never see each other or meet in person.

At a loss for words I said nothing. Luna continued. "There is an author who lives in your country, somewhere in London I believe, who is much attuned to Pixies, Faeries, and the mystical spirit world as well. He too, clearly hears their song. I would not at all be surprised if, in the future, he writes books on the subject. His name is Arthur Conan Doyle. Have you heard of him?"

I did not know what to say. The ethereal, enchanting music Sherlock had played earlier, was beyond anything I had heard from him previously, but this talk of Pixies was difficult to accept. Of course, I was hearing it directly from a mermaid, so it did lend a good deal of credibility to the idea of a spirit world.

At that moment Captain Nemo entered the chamber to inform us we were approaching the area where the ship would be intercepted. He wanted to impart to Luna the details on how the plan would unfold.

With a pang in my heart, I said goodbye to Luna and the Captain, and I left the airlock chamber to join Sherlock in his "pondering" on the communication break. I entered the salon and found him eating spoonfuls of seaweed tea directly from the tea pot and saying aloud, "No! No! No! It just cannot be!"

He looked up and offered me a spoonful of the odd smelling, mushy green substance commenting, "Hello Watson. Did you know that, in addition to making outstanding tranquilizers and knockout gas, there are types of seaweed that make excellent beverages to improve mental focus and clarity of thought? Not to mention the outstanding energy boost you get from it. I discovered if I just eat the seaweed directly, it works even better. It does not taste like much, though. I believe that someday someone will sell these beverages as a mental boost drink. I can see it now. *Dr. Watson's Miracle, Monster, Seaweed Mind Elixir, Guaranteed to improve your focus or your money back!* What do say old boy?"

I looked at him incredulously and asked, "So you have determined the source of the communication breech? You cannot hide it from me, Holmes, I know you too well."

He set the spoon down and looked at me intensely and replied, "Yes, you do know me very well. I have an idea, but I am not one hundred percent certain. It is too unlikely and too inconceivable, Watson. It is simply too impossible to believe just yet. When I have eliminated all of the other possibilities, every single one of them, then I will know for certain, however improbable it may be. Then I will let you know."

Chapter 18. A Most Unusual Way to Stop an Auxiliary Steam Ship, (But it went quite well, all things considered.)

Captain Nemo entered the salon to inform us that the chartered vessel had finally been sighted, and we were ready to intercept them. He had been cruising at the surface level of the ocean with the control bridge viewing ports above water to be able to search in all directions for them, while still keeping the *Nautilus* in a low profile. When the vessel had been sighted, the *Nautilus* immediately submerged to remain hidden from view. The Captain had determined their heading and was following the same course they were, except underwater. The Nautilus pulled ahead of the vessel to provide the distance required, adjusted the depth, and Luna exited the airlock chamber with the cork-tethered explosive charges. We were able to watch her from the aft facing windows in the steering room. Everything seemed to be going well. The first float had been released and was nearing the surface as the vessel quickly churned its way towards us. Luna adjusted her location to the port side, released the second float, and immediately dove deeper to get away from the forthcoming explosions no matter how small they were to be. We could hear the rhythmic pulsing of the paddle wheels as it approached the proximity of the tethered explosive charges. The visibility in the clear water was exceptional, but the float was so small, it was hard to see just what was happening. Sherlock, looking at his watch and counting, stated, "Based on the length of the tethers and the speed of the ship, we should hear the first charge... detonate... right about..." As he said the word "Now!" we heard a muffled explosion as the first charge detonated, and we saw the starboard paddle wheel disintegrate. The entire vessel shook slightly and lurched as it lost the driving force of the wheel. A moment later, the port paddle wheel shattered into splinters as the second charge went off.

Sherlock clasped his hands together, sighed, and stated, "Yes. Precisely as I calculated. The paddle wheels caught the floats and pulled the charges right up to the paddles with no harm to the hull. That is sterling."

The twin paddle wheels had been destroyed, and there was a rain of wood and debris that drifted down from the vessel as it continued on its course using only the stern propeller. Their speed was significantly reduced, but it was still making progress. We could only wonder what their reaction was on board, as they realized the loss of both side wheels. The *Nautilus* was suspended motionless in the depths, while we waited for Luna to return to the airlock chamber. The vessel passed directly over head, with remnants of the paddle wheels still drifting downward. Along with the slowly sinking debris, we noticed projectiles streaking past at high speeds. They acted like rifle bullets that had been fired into the water. Apparently the crew of the vessel was along the railing firing in to the depths. The clarity of the water was relatively decent in that part of the ocean, and they may have seen the mass of the *Nautilus*'s hull and thought it to be a sea monster of some sort. They would certainly have a whale of a tale to tell when they returned.

Their rifle bullets could not harm the *Nautilus*. However, Luna was still somewhere out in the surrounding seas, and she could possibly be injured. The Captain increased the depth of the ship to take us out of their range and provide more protection to Luna as she returned to the vessel. The hull of the *Nautilus* would provide an excellent shield. I left the bridge and hurried to the airlock chamber so I would know the moment she had safely returned.

With growing concern I paced back and forth along the side of the pool as I waited for her. I wondered if she had been injured by the concussion from the charges, or perhaps she had been struck by a stray bullet. Finally, I sat down on the rim and stared intently into the entry pool. To my great relief, she came bursting out of the pool literally into my arms, of course soaking me with sea water for the third time.

"Why John, you were worried about me again. That is so sweet of you." Much to my surprise and no small pleasure, she then kissed me on the cheek and slid back into the pool, saying "I am fine. Now quickly go tell the Captain I am back on board the *Nautilus*, so he can go after the steam ship. We must 'seas' the day. We cannot let them escape." Once again, I was dripping with salt water as I worked my way back to the bridge to let Captain Nemo and Sherlock know Luna was safely aboard the *Nautilus*.

Captain Nemo thanked me and stated that we would now continue after the vessel to disable the stern propeller. Looking me up and down, Sherlock appraised me and asked, "What did you do, Watson, jump in after her to go swim along with her? You know, if you two continue to go on meeting like this, you will need to lay in a good supply of towels and cold medicine. You had better stay away from the Captain's Persian rugs."

I looked at him, asked if he had any messages with invisible ink writing to be revealed, wrung the salt water out of my sleeve onto the floor in front of him, and left to change into dry clothing.

I returned to my cabin to change clothes yet again, while Captain Nemo commenced his pursuit of the vessel. Constantly adjusting speed, course and depth, while avoiding rifle and small cannon fire, the Captain and his crew were flawless in their maneuvering of the *Nautilus*. With a doctor's precision, he used the ramming spur to damage their rudder and propeller without harming the hull whatsoever. We retreated a distance from the vicinity to observe them and verify that, while they had lost propulsion, they were still safe and seaworthy. We had thought that, without use of their paddle wheels and propeller, they would be stranded, but they immediately commenced to put out a jury-rigged rudder and set all the sail they could. It seemed as if they were determined to reach that island.

Since the vessel was a steam auxiliary, she carried sail in addition to their steam engine, and they were hoisting all the canvas they could. Captain Nemo observed that while the *Nautilus* was very effective against paddle wheels and propellers, and if we wanted to sink it outright, against the hull itself, he could do very little against the sails.

Sherlock observed the vessel under sail and replied to Captain Nemo's observation, "That may not be the case. It just so happens that I have recently written a paper *"Practical Applications for Catapults, Trebuchets, Mangonels, and Other Non-Explosive Powered Ballistic Devices"*. We could use a catapult to launch small explosive charges into their sails and rigging. Nothing too powerful, just enough to destroy their masts. I could design something quite quickly, and your crew could assemble it with what you have on board. We will have to wait until dark to deploy it since we must be close enough to reach them, which, by the way, will put us in range of their gun fire."

Captain Nemo sighed and with an incredulous smile asked, "With all of the modern technology on board the Nautilus at our disposal, you are suggesting we employ a device that dates back to ancient history?"

Sherlock nodded and replied, "It dates back to 339 BC to be exact, and it has been quite effective over the centuries. Of course, the trebuchet is the most effective type of catapult. In the 1304 siege of Sterling Castle, they deployed a massive trebuchet called *Warwolf*, which, with a single 300 pound shot, leveled an entire section of the castle wall, effectively ending the siege. In fact, when the castle defenders saw it being assembled, they were so intimidated, they tried to surrender, but Edward I of England refused their surrender because he wanted to witness for himself the destructive power of the weapon. Of course, we do not require anything that large. It took thirty wagons just to transport the materials to build the machine, and three months to assemble it. I only need something simple that can launch the explosive devices from the deck of the *Nautilus* into their rigging to bring down the masts."

"That is a paramount concept," Captain Nemo replied, "The *Nautilus* is at your disposal."

Within a short while, Holmes had come up with a workable catapult that could launch small charges at their sails. They lashed spare parts together to make the frame and mounted a metal bowl to the end of a pole for the launching arm. When I informed Luna of the plan, she laughingly commented that, at the rate Sherlock was using up the Captains metal bowls from the galley, there would be none left for cooking, and she was quite 'bowled' over.

Per Sherlock's direction, we would mount the catapult on the deck, aft of the raised steering and observation bridge, to provide as much protection as possible for him and the crew members who would be assisting him.

The Captain informed us there had been only enough material left to make four charges, since we had previously used the same materials for the explosives that had damaged the paddle wheels. The catapult would have to be accurate.

Sherlock confidently replied, "Using navigation instruments on board, I have calculated the distance between the *Nautilus* and the other ship, the relative speed of both vessels, the height of the masts, the angle of the firing arm when the charge is released, the force with which it will hit the cross bar, the weight of the charge, the wind speed and direction, the wave height, and the current. I assure you, my calculations are altogether accurate, and I will only need two of them; one for each mast."

I looked at him with a smile and said, "Sherlock, I am impressed, but did you check air temperature and relative humidity?'

Sherlock looked at me and answered, "Indeed. They are both factored into the calculation, as is the barometric pressure and the salinity of the ocean."

With darkness as our ally and all interior lighting extinguished, the *Nautilus* quietly drew up a stern of the sailing vessel. All of us held our breath to avoid any noise as Sherlock prepared the catapult. He signaled he was ready to launch the explosive charge from the bowl at the end of the firing arm. He waited for the exact moment, gave the command to release, and the charge made a perfect ark into the mizzen topsail, where it detonated and brought down the mizzen mast. While Sherlock and the

Nautilus crew rewound the strap that provided the tension and reloaded the bowl, the crew of the vessel we were pursuing assembled at the stern rail with rifles and began firing at us. In the dark, they could not see well and their shots went astray or bounced harmlessly off the *Nautilus*'s hull. Again Sherlock gave the command, and the second charge was launched, this time destroying the main mast. As the wreckage of the masts and rigging collapsed to the deck, the vessel lost all forward momentum and came to a halt. They had finally been stopped and we could resume our course to the Azores.

Before we did, however, Captain Nemo produced a small iron chest, and per his request, Sherlock launched it at the vessel, dropping it squarely on to the deck. "That should cover the damage to their vessel." The Captain stated with satisfaction. "It is not their fault they took on the passengers they did."

Sherlock nodded and asserted, "I would think so. The gold coins in that chest can most certainly purchase a brand new vessel, and more."

"And I also included a note to the owner of the vessel," said the Captain, "to subdue and restrain his passengers until authorities arrive to tow them back to port and safely relieve them of their dangerous guests."

Chapter 19. A Most Unusual Solution,
(And it's amazing what a good cup of tea can do.)

The makeshift catapult had been disassembled and stowed, the *Nautilus* had submerged and we were back on course to the Azores. We had all gathered again in the salon, and Luna was once more in her water chair, translating as needed. Jules Verne complimented Sherlock on his clever idea and reiterated that not all solutions need be based on futuristic technology. He asked what the plan would be when we arrived at their final base, since we did not know what to expect or what resources they might have available.

Against the background noise of the *Nautilus* engines running at full speed, Captain Nemo responded, "That is true, we are taking a risk in going there, but I feel it is worth it if we can strand a large portion of their group and incapacitate them. Success at their final base, along with our Iceland victory would eliminate the majority of their organization. The only question remaining is the source of the communication breech in England." Then turning to Holmes he asked, "Have you made any more progress on that Sherlock?"

Holmes distractedly looked up from the papers and material he was working with and mumbled, "Eliminating possibilities, Captain Nemo, eliminating possibilities. It is really quite elementary, but at the same time most demanding and time consuming."

Luna looked askance and asked, "But how can it be easy and difficult at the same time? Is that not like saying it won't take long at all, only as long as it takes?"

"That's it precisely!" exclaimed Sherlock. "You are quite perceptive. The deductive process itself is very straight forward and simple, but it is time consuming to do a proper and thorough job of it. I must look at every single possibility."

I thought to myself, "Yes, Sherlock, and even the ones you don't want to see." Something in his behavior and attitude had changed since he had begun working on that problem. Normally, Sherlock worked with a cold, emotionless determination that was dedicated but detached. This particular problem seemed to have touched a nerve with him, as if he had found the answer but would not accept it. It was as if he had to keep working at it to find an alternative solution that was more agreeable. I wondered what it was that he could not accept.

Captain Nemo, returning the discussion to what we would do when we arrived, turned to Luna and said, "You have overheard them talk about this last base. It is located somewhere in the Azores. There are nine major islands in the group, divided into three smaller groups. If I showed you a chart of the Azores, do you think you could determine which one of them it might be? That would be most helpful."

With a smile and laugh, she answered, "Well Captain, 'eel' see what I can do. I did hear something about the odd shape of the island and the excellent wine found there."

Jules Verne looked up and stated, "That would be the island of Sao Jorge, or Saint George. It is very long and slender with many steep cliffs along its coast. It was once noted for its fine quality wine. I had an opportunity to try some at the 1867 World Exposition in Paris. It was quite excellent. It is sad that a grape disease has struck the island. The wine making enterprise there was devastated. It is all but gone."

"My question is," stated the Captain, "where can they be hiding their base? I know those islands are very remote, but there is a small population there. How can they avoid being seen? Do you think it is another underwater base? I cannot imagine that they have too many more submersibles. We have already eliminated four of them. I would think that their airship would be noticeable, even in a place as remote as that."

Sherlock set down his writing implement, looked up, and sharply stated, "It is senseless to speculate. We must wait and see what turns up when we arrive. Only when we have gathered all the facts, can we determine what it is the facts tell us, and whether or not it is true or false. The information we currently have is: 1. They have a base there. 2. Following the example of their other bases, it is most likely well hidden. 3. The island is small, remote, and features tall cliffs. 4. There is a native population on the island. 5. Not that it has any bearing at all on the subject, they make good wine. Tell me, what conclusion can we draw from that without further information? Now, if you will excuse me, I will be in my quarters. And Captain, if I may borrow your violin." With that, Holmes stood up, collected the violin case, and left the salon.

It is known, Holmes has a reputation for being odd, eccentric, and at times arrogant, but this was unusual even for him.

Luna watched him as he left and commented, "His mood is worse than a school of tuna that has been stranded on the beach after a high tide and left in the sun to bake for a week. Is he unhappy or upset about something? Perhaps the Captain could prepare a nice sautéed sea urchin and pickled herring casserole to cheer him up."

We cringed at the thought of Luna's suggestion, but before anyone could answer, the sound of violin music began to echo through the *Nautilus* -- a sad, haunting melody.

I commented to Luna, "He has been working on locating the communication breech in the Atlantean network, and something about it has been bothering him. He can get very involved in his calculations and deductions, and at times he may get too tense."

Luna smiled brightly and asked, "What kind of tents, wigwams or tepees?" and then she laughed at her word play, and added, "What he needs is a good cup of the right kind of seaweed tea."

Just then the violin music stopped abruptly, and Sherlock came rushing back into the salon with a very satisfied look on his face and cheerfully stated. "I have figured it out. What I need right now is a good cup of the right kind of seaweed tea. Captain, may I have access to your dried seaweed stores and one of the laboratories on board?"

I thought to myself, "Now, is that the ultimate in irony, or am I as soggy as Luna's ocean metaphors?"

Pleased to see the positive change in him the Captain readily agreed, and Sherlock exited the salon whistling the tune *Tea for Two*. I was at a complete loss as to what had just happened but I was glad to see he had resolved his concern.

We continued on course, uncertain of what we would find, while Sherlock spent all of his time in the *Nautilus*'s laboratory working with the dried seaweed. I checked in on him once, to see how he was doing, and he considered me and asked, "Who are you? Do I know you?"

I looked at him in surprise and replied, "Sherlock, It's me John Watson! Of course you know me."

He looked closer at me and responded, "Oh yes, yes, I do, don't I? This is excellent. Just excellent! Perfect timing, Watson, old boy. Carry on." He returned to his work so engrossed he did not even know I was there.

I left the laboratory with several more questions than what I had when I entered. I found Luna back in the entry pool chamber and asked if she had any idea as to what was going on with Sherlock.

She laughed and said it seemed 'fishy' to her, but she did not want to be 'shellfish', so she explained, "His mood is like the tide: It went out and left him stranded. He was left high and dry so to speak, with no place to turn. But then the tide came back in and refloated him, so now all is well. He is back on course."

I looked at her luminous face with outright confusion, and asked if she could please explain without using ocean metaphors. Luna laughed and said, "I of course I 'cod' do that. He has come to a realization about what is troubling him, and accepted it. And in doing so, he has come up with a solution to the problem. That is what he is working on in the laboratory. You will see. Everything will be fine. He will be as happy as a wet clam. And I do know firsthand how happy clams are when they are wet.

"Luna," I commented, "I am pleased to see you seem much happier now than when we first met. Your humorous, lighthearted nature is delightful."

"That is because Monsieur Verne has been rescued and is now safe. I was so concerned for him. He is not in good health, and those people are terribly cruel. When you and I first met, my only concern was freeing him. It was like a dark cloud of octopus ink hanging over me. But now my ocean is full of sunfish, and of course star fish, and moon snails, and rainbow guppies, and…"

I just smiled and listened as she continued listing a multitude of different sea creatures, while in the background the haunting organ music of Captain Nemo filled the *Nautilus*.

Chapter 20. A Most Unusual Situation,
(And some excellent wine.)

We had arrived at Sao Jorge Island, surfaced, and observed it from a distance. Tall cliffs protruded out of the sea, as waves crashed against them relentlessly. The verdant green vegetation of the island stood in contrast to the vibrant azure blue of the ocean. A flock of sea birds cavorted and soared near the shore. Nothing seemed out of the ordinary. We commenced a circumnavigation of the island, looking for something that did not seem right. We had almost completed rounding Sao Jorge, when Sherlock pointed out a large building near the water located in proximity to a small harbor. It had two smoke stacks on the landward side, and the seaward side came close to the water where two large doors could be opened to allow objects to slide into the harbor. It looked like a facility for constructing vessels of some kind. Captain Nemo pointed out that the last time he had been near this island, it had not been there.

As we observed the building, we noticed two men in dark uniforms and tall boots patrolling the shore. The low profile of the *Nautilus* in the water prevented them from seeing us, but we quickly retreated out of sight and submerged. The enemy was there and blatantly out in the open. That made for an interesting situation. Captain Nemo stated that before proceeding any further, he wanted to scout the perimeter of the island underwater. The Azores are known to be of volcanic origin with many caves and caverns. There might be an underwater entrance to a hidden lagoon.

We cautiously followed the shoreline and the cliffs, being wary of the surging tide near the rocks and shallows. On several occasions, the *Nautilus* started to enter a cave only to discover it to be a dead end and had to retreat back out in reverse. The Captain's skills in helmsmanship and navigation were impressive. On and on we went until we had completed our search of the island's perimeter. We found no underwater access or entrance to the interior. We decided to wait for nightfall to investigate the large building we had discovered near the shore.

Darkness fell, and the *Nautilus* was positioned not far from land in a deserted area of the coast, yet as close to the large building as we dared. Using a variety of items found aboard the ship, Sherlock, who is a master in the art of altering ones appearance, created disguises that would allow us to blend in with the local islanders. The Captain spoke Portuguese and French, while Sherlock understood French and German, so we hoped to find out what in fact was going on there. We utilized the launch from the *Nautilus* to make our way to the beach and then hid the craft and ourselves from view.

From our hidden location, we observed the islanders for a period and noticed a sadness and fear in them, as if their lives had been drained of all hope. We continued to watch, until we spied an older gentleman who appeared to be a farmer, walking along the path. We casually walked out into the pathway as well, and the Captain pleasantly greeted him. He looked up at Captain Nemo, appraised him, and replied, "Hello, my friend. In spite of your native attire, I see that you are not from this island." Then staring intently into Captain Nemo's eyes, he continued. "Forgive me if I stare at you. You remind me of my son whom I recently lost. I do not sense danger from you. But this is a dangerous place. What brings you and your companions to Sao Jorge?"

The Captain bowed his head and said he was sorry to hear of the gentleman's loss, and we were curious regarding the very large building near the harbor, as it had certainly not been here on his previous visit to this pleasant island.

The man looked at the building, sighed, and said it was both a blessing and a curse. Sherlock assured him that we meant no harm and asked if there was somewhere safe we could talk. And perhaps we could help him.

He looked at us as if to determine if we could be trusted, glanced to the right and the left, nodded his head, and asked us to follow him. His home was only a short distance away, and we could see that, at one time his property had been a vineyard but the surrounding vines were all withered and dead. The home while simple, indicated that the owner had been well off in earlier times when the vineyard was prosperous. Now there was a sparseness to it that conveyed a sense of loss.

Seated inside his home, at a rustic wooden table, he offered each of us a glass of the island's wine. He stated that, once the wine was gone there would be no more, as the grapes had all been killed by a disease. He was obviously happy to share the last of his wine with us. He said he could see goodness in us, as compared to those who ran the factory in the large building.

"Have you seen what they build in there?" The Captain asked.

The old man shook his head, "I have not been inside myself, as I am too old to work in there, but those who have say they build boats that look like whales, and they swim underwater like whales. That sounds unbelievable, but it is true. You must believe me. And the factory owners treat the workers like slaves. The conditions are truly terrible. When they first arrived and said they were bringing work to the island, everyone welcomed them. We are very remote here, and there was no other work after the grapes started dying. The island men were happy to get jobs, but then we realized how cruel these people are. My son tried to stand up to them but he was killed. They said it was an accident, but I know better. I believe they killed him to set an example. No one has dared to question them since he died. We are like prisoners on our own island. Is there anything you can do to help us?"

Captain Nemo shook the man's hand and assured him saying, "That is why we are here, to stop this organization and free you from their grasp. How many people of that group are on the island? Can you tell me where they are at this time?"

Sherlock then added, "Sir, it is most important. Can you tell me how many of these whale vessels they have built?"

We learned from the farmer, that there were only ten members of the organization still remaining on the island, and the islanders provide all the labor in the factory and work under the cruelest of conditions. Four of the whale vessels had been built and had left the island, while a fifth was nearing completion. He did not know where they went when they left. He did know, at night, the members of the organization all stayed together in a smaller structure behind the main work building, except for those who patrolled the area. Usually two guards were on patrol around the factory building all night long.

We learned what else we could, thanked him for his help, and told him that we would be back momentarily to deal with the factory owners. We returned to the *Nautilus* to collect the two remaining explosive charges, more of the seaweed knockout gas, several of Nemo's crewmen, and my service revolver just in case. Our plan was to surprise the exterior guards, render them unconscious, and then use the knockout gas on the remainder of the group in the small building so they could be locked up, and removed from the island permanently. The factory and submersible were to be destroyed.

We made our way toward the factory area, found the first guard, and with Sherlock in his disguise providing a distraction, I was able to surprise and disarm the guard with a solid right hook. Captain Nemo and his crewman had dispatched the second guard, and soon, we had them both tied up. Sherlock discretely peered through the dust-covered windows of the smaller building that contained the remainder of the foe to determine our best approach based on the location of members of the group inside. It turned out that simply opening the front door, throwing both canisters inside, and closing the door was the indeed the most logical approach. As we waited for the seaweed knockout gas to take effect, Sherlock grinned and said, "Well Watson, once again, the simplest approach is the best. That seaweed based knockout gas has proven to be most effective. I shall have to update my paper on the subject when we return.

It did indeed prove to be most effective. When we entered the building, every one of the descendants of Mu were unconscious. With the help of the *Nautilus* crew, as well as several men from the island who came to assist us once they realized what had occurred, the entire group of Mu descendants were restrained and transported to the island jail. We explained to the islanders that foreign authorities would later arrive to take the prisoners away. The islanders were most grateful and thanked us profusely.

The only task now remaining was the destruction of the factory building and final submersible. Captain Nemo and Sherlock first examined the workings of the factory and its machinery and were very impressed. The Captain made mental notes on various subjects pertaining to their technology. The sophistication of it all was far beyond anything existing in London. Captain Nemo noted the world, as it is, was not yet ready for such futuristic science. We placed the explosive charges, retreated to a safe location, detonated the devices, and eliminated the last remnant of the Mu technology. The island men who had helped us, cheered as the factory was destroyed but then looked at each other as if wondering what to do next.

Realizing the islanders were once again at a loss for work, since their grapes had succumbed to disease, Captain Nemo assigned two of his crew, a biologist and a botanist, to help the islanders develop a new crop they could grow and harvest there. He had a feeling that oranges would do quite well in this climate, and provided them with what they needed to get started. He assured them he would be back to see how they succeeded and to pick up his two crewmen. They thanked us again for coming to their rescue and insisted we accept several bottles of their excellent wine. Now we were bound for England, and, at last, the mysterious source of the Atlantean communication breech would be revealed.

Chapter 21. Another Most Unusual Plan,
(And I think Sherlock is still being vague.)

Once we were back on board the *Nautilus*, we gathered again in the salon with Luna in her water chair, and we related to Jules Verne, and Luna, who had stayed behind, the events that had transpired on the island. We explained how the Mu descendants had utilized their advanced technology to build the submersibles using the forced labor of the remote and isolated islanders. Jules Verne thought about it and commented, "That would be an intriguing subject for a novel, but I think I would place the events in a *City in the Sahara* far out in the desert. It is even more remote out there."

Luna frowned and asked how he would explain the whale submersibles out in the desert. "Is that not like a fish out of the water?" she laughingly asked.

He just waved his hand and said, "Submersible vessels in the shape of whales? No one would accept that. It is too strange even for fiction. I will have them use helicopter-planes." Then with a wink he added, "Whale submersibles are almost as impossible to believe in as mermaids."

Luna laughed and whisked her tail to splash a small amount of water at him and said, "'Whale' see about that." Then changing the subject she added, "So what is our plan when we get to London? Without a proper plan, we really will be like a fish out of water, and you know what that smells like after several days."

Sherlock cleared his throat, paused a moment to get our attention, and answered. "Friends, things are not always as they seem. Several of the facts that we thought we knew before we arrived at Sao Jorge turned out to be not quite as we believed. We knew there was a Mu base there, but it was much more than just a base. It was a fully operational factory. We believed it would be well hidden. It was not in the least bit hidden; it was out in plain sight. And the wine, or lack of it, did actually have something to do with the situation. What that tells us is that what we think we know is not always what we really know. You do know what I mean, don't you?"

We all stared at him in silence, except for Luna who brightly asked, "Is that like the wisdom of the sealed oyster that reveals no pearl? I have always believed that it is quite obvious, as clear as a cod fish on a kelp bed."

Not even attempting to translate or answer Luna's sea life metaphor, Sherlock went on, "What I am trying to say is I believe I know precisely where the breech in communication is, but I am not one hundred percent certain. If it is as I suspect, I already have a plan in place on how to effectively treat it. If it is not as I suspect, I will not be overly saddened, but then we shall have to keep looking, which will be a challenge. To make the final determination, I shall need your help to execute my plan.

"When we arrive in London, Watson, you, Jules Verne, and Luna shall come with me..."

When she heard this, Luna conspicuously sloshed water with her tail and asked, "Excuse me, and how indeed are we to do that? It is not as if I can swim down the boulevard, unless you are planning to flood all of London. That would be more exciting than playing croquet with puffer fish for croquet balls and hammer head sharks for mallets."

Sherlock answered, "Why it is most elementary. We humans have special suits made of waterproof fabric that holds the water out to keep us dry when we are breathing underwater. That same material can be made into a flexible, comfortable skirt to hold water in around Luna's tail as she sits in a wheeled chair with a blanket over the lower half of her body. It will look quite normal to anyone; just a lady in a wheelchair with a blanket over her legs."

Luna flashed a radiant smile and exclaimed, "What a delightful idea! I will get to see the surface world up close without even having to flood London. I thought that idea was all wet! Maybe someday I could even use the chair to come and visit John Watson for afternoon tea." Then with a coy grin, she added, "but Mr. Holmes, why do you call it "elementary?" I don't understand at all what it has to do with a tree that grows the twelfth, thirteenth and fourteenth letters of the alphabet."

Confused, Captain Nemo looked at Luna oddly, and she answered with the brightest smile, "An "L","M","N" tree!"

Sherlock shook his head and asked her, "Have you by any chance met the Cheshire Cat from Wonderland?"

She thought a moment and replied, "No, I can't say that I have. But I have met several catfish, a few dog fish, and even a cowardly lion fish, but none of them went by the name of 'Cheshire'."

Holmes ignored her humor and went on. "Now as I was saying: Watson, Jules Verne, and Luna will come with me to a certain government building at 10:45 AM. Captain Nemo, at precisely 11:00 AM, you will send a message to your fellow Atlantean who is positioned in the British government. I will provide you the message. If the breech is where I believe it is, we shall see the results first hand. I will respond accordingly, and if my new tea formula works as expected, our problem shall be resolved. Any questions?"

I immediately asked him why he felt it necessary for Luna to be there and if she would be in any great danger.

He casually replied, "Of course not, Watson. I would not ask her to come along, if there was any more danger than disabling hostile submersibles, airships, or steam auxiliary ships."

Luna replied cheerfully, "That is wonderful. I am skilled in all of those tasks. I am as ready to assist as an octopus is to arm wrestle."

"We will not need your skills in those activities, Luna," Sherlock answered, "but I will need you to translate for Jules Verne and possibly to emphasize a point in a way that only you could do."

Captain Nemo looked at Sherlock and asked, "If this plan of yours works, then the communication breech in our Atlantean network shall be sealed, correct?"

Sherlock replied, "Not only the breech, but if I am correct, the resources that have been supplying the descendants of Mu. After we had determined the location of the communication leak was in London, it was wise that you contacted your agents in other governments to apprehend the Mu criminals that we left in Iceland and the Azores, as well as those on the disabled chartered vessel. They will be incarcerated and will no longer be a threat to the world. Now we have only one person left to deal with."

While Sherlock was speaking, I noticed that he had been holding what looked like a coin in his hand and moving it back and forth. When he finished his statement, he flipped it in the air, caught it, and put it in his pocket. It was then I noticed it was the round disk that Captain Nemo had found aboard the *Saint-Michel III* when Jules Verne had gone missing. It was the one with the star map, compass, and stylized letter "M".

The remainder of the voyage to London was rather sad for me. I was pleased that we had rescued Jules Verne and stopped the descendants of Mu in their plans for world domination. And I was happy that Sherlock seemed quite satisfied with his plans to resolve the breech in the Atlanteans communication network. But once this adventure was concluded and we were back in our flat in London, that meant I would probably never see Luna again. As disappointing as that was, I did not want to express my feelings, as she seemed so very happy and excited about the prospect of seeing the surface world in a new way from the special wheeled chair and water containment skirt that the *Nautilus* crew was fabricating. I told myself not to worry about it now and to be satisfied with what time we still had together and make the most of it. And so, I gazed at her endless beauty and enjoyed her playful wit and charm in silence.

Chapter 22. A Most Unusual Confrontation,
(And it turns out a good cup of tea is the answer.)

The time to commence our final plan had at last arrived. We had returned to London, and using an empty, abandoned pier in a remote section of the waterfront, secretly disembarked from the *Nautilus* under the cover of darkness. We made our way to the home of Captain Nemo's Atlantean counterpart in London and waited for daylight. Sherlock and I were dressed in Mu uniforms and boots, which he had taken from the factory before it was destroyed, and we darkened our hair and wore thin mustaches. He explained it was all a part of his plan, and that at the right moment, we would bring Jules Verne and Luna into a particular government office, and the answer would be revealed. Many times in the past, without explaining anything in advance, Sherlock had planned out grandiose and elaborate ruses with great flair to expose a villain, and I assumed this again was one of his grand theatrical masterpieces.

As we traveled to the government buildings, I pushed the wheeled chair that held Luna and her water skirt, which was safely concealed under a thick woolen blanket. She expressed surprise and amazement at the wonders of the surface world. As two large clusters of people crossed a busy thoroughfare trying to avoid the horse-drawn hansoms and growlers, she commented it was like watching two schools of herring trying to avoid a pod of dolphins at feeding time. Jules Verne, who was walking next to her, laughed when she translated her comment, and he explained some of the various things they saw along the way. Sherlock checked his pocket watch and said it was time to execute his plan.

While I was still at a loss as to where we were going, Sherlock knew the way unerringly. The government buildings are a large complex crowded with people coming and going, but Holmes guided us through it and eventually led us down a long corridor to an unmarked door and had us stop. People looked at us in our uniforms, with the elderly Jules Verne and Luna in her wheeled chair, but no one said anything. Sherlock checked his watch again, looked at us and stated, "Captain Nemo's message has been delivered to his government counterpart. Now we wait."

The British Government routinely employs numerous messengers to relay communications and documents between agencies and offices, and it was typically done with the usual stoic manner and sluggish steady pace of that level of employee. The halls had been filled with delivery boys slowly and resolutely carrying their notes from one office to the next.

We had not waited long, however, when an uncharacteristic and out of breath messenger came rushing up to the office where we had been waiting. His entire nature was different from the other couriers. There was an air of urgency about him and his task. He was about to enter the office, when Sherlock stepped directly in front of him, quickly glanced at the message in the boy's hand, and said, "Excuse me, my good fellow. We are going in to see Mycroft Holmes right this minute. I can take that in for you. Your note actually pertains to my companions and I. Now I am sure you are quite busy and have many other messages to deliver. Here is a thank you, for your efforts." Sherlock then handed the messenger two shillings, deftly removed the note from the boys hand and urged him on his way.

I could not believe it! Mycroft Holmes was the source of the communication breech! It was no wonder Sherlock was so upset after he had determined who it was. That must have been a devastating realization. From what he had told me about his brother, Mycroft Holmes was an integral part of the British government At times, he was the British government. Why would he be involved in something like this? What was going on here? Where was this unusual adventure heading next?

Sherlock, with the note in his hand, opened the door and with a brusque attitude ushered us into the office. It was large, elegant, and cluttered with books, papers, and maps. A tea service stood on a small table off in the corner. The walls were lined with book shelves, and there was a large walnut desk in the center of the room. Behind the desk sat an equally large, heavily built man whose brow was raised and showed signs of great intellect.

His suit, while of excellent quality, was unkempt as if he simply could not be bothered to spend the effort required to maintain his appearance. This was Mycroft Holmes, Sherlock's brother.

Taking the lead and in a disguised voice, Sherlock handed Mycroft the note, casually threw the medallion with the star map, compass, and stylized "M" on the desk, and said, "Here is your latest message. Your delivery boy seems to be a bit lax and slow today. This message tells you to expect two envoys from Mu, that we have the code medallion for identification, and that we are bringing Jules Verne and his lady interpreter to your office for a visit. He only speaks French you know. But we are already here. Imagine that! We have finally convinced Jules Verne to share with you the secret of how he travels in time. Now at last, the weapons of the future will be available for the good of The Empire."

Mycroft shifted in his chair and replied, "That is excellent news. It will be of immense help to Great Britain and to the descendants of Mu as well, but why did you chance bringing him here to my office? That is taking an unnecessary risk. I have kept this association between the descendants of Mu and myself secret for a reason. I agreed to fund the rebuilding of Mu culture as well as the reestablishment of your science and technology. Your people agreed to use it for the good of the British Empire, and to gain the secret of time travel from Jules Verne. With that ability we can obtain weapons from the future, but the agreement was to be kept a secret. No one else in the government knows what I am doing here. Not even my own brother knows."

Sherlock quickly pulled off his fake mustache, and in his own voice stated, "I would not say that, dear brother. But my question is, Why? Why are you doing this?"

Mycroft's eyes grew wide with astonishment as he realized it was his brother who stood before him, and he exclaimed, "Sherlock, what on earth are you doing here? And how did you find out about this? Do you have any idea what you have done? You have interrupted an important plan to bring power and security to the British Empire. The world is heading towards a great war. With my knowledge and insight, I can see the inevitable results as clear as day. Not this decade, nor the next, but eventually the whole world will be at war. It will be devastating. The weapons of the future would have protected Great Britain. Why would you, of all people, want to prevent that?"

Sherlock looked at his brother and shook his head. "Mycroft, you have more knowledge, facts, information, and insight than anyone in the world, but you have been so blind. The organization that you have foolishly associated yourself with has no intention of sharing the weapons of the future with anyone. I do not know how you met or came to be working together, but the populace of the lost city of Mu has been striving towards only one goal since ancient times, and that is world domination. We have seen the result of their activities in the Azores. They enslaved the islanders to build their ships. They have no regard for human life whatsoever."

Taking the initiative, Luna leaned forward and addressed Mycroft. "It is true what your brother says. These people are evil and without remorse. They have cruelly used their submersible vessels to sink countless ships with hundreds of innocent lives lost. I have seen it with my own eyes more times than I care to remember."

Mycroft looked at Luna with scorn and asked, "And who are you that I should believe you? How could you have seen them sink all those ships you say they have destroyed? You are sitting there in that chair and telling me that you have witnessed them sinking countless ships? The next thing you will be telling me is that you are a mermaid who swims the seven seas, and you saw it firsthand."

Luna let her blanket fall to the floor, and pushing up against the arms of the wheeled chair, she lifted her lower body from the water skirt, to fully reveal her luminescent scaly green tail.

"I assure you sir, I have seen it with my own eyes. And yes, I am a mermaid! For emphasis, she flourished her tail and drenched Mycroft with saltwater.

Sherlock's brother was completely stunned. As well as soaking wet, Mycroft was speechless. It was not surprising really, as Luna does have that effect on people. I would actually say, he was more shocked discovering she was a mermaid, than when he realized it was his brother Sherlock, who was standing in front of him moments ago.

"She...she's a mermaid! Sherlock where did you find her? How did you find her? It's impossible! I have had people searching the world over for creatures like her. You remember our childhood wager? That if mermaids really exist, I would find one before you did." He stared intently at Luna and exclaimed, "Who are you? What are you doing here?"

While slowly moving her tail back and forth in her water skirt, she glared back at him and exclaimed, "Why you barnacle encrusted, slimy, sea slug! I am helping your brother stop a threat to your world as well as mine. The pack you are running with has killed hundreds of people. Don't you see that? Or as Sherlock said, are you too blinded by your facts and information?" She then undulated her tail and splashed him again.

Holmes replied, "Yes, Mycroft, she is a mermaid, and not one to argue with. Our age-old bet is unimportant now. That is not the question. I want to know how you intercepted the Atlanteans communications."

He dismissively waved his hand and said, "Sherlock, you know that all information in the government comes to me and goes through my office. I am privy to everything. Nothing happens in this administration that I am not aware of. Your Atlantean friends have a highly placed official in our government, but I am sure you knew that. I noticed some odd messages coming through to him in an incomprehensible language. It got my attention. I usually do not like to expend any more effort than is absolutely required, but this was intriguing.

Actually, it was you who helped me decode it, brother. Your paper on deciphering ancient languages was most useful. Although I did have to write you a letter for clarification on one point. Of course, it came from an ancient language scholar, and not me.

"This gave me insight regarding the Atlanteans who have been monitoring us, as well as to what Jules Verne was doing with time travel. About the same time, I was contacted by the survivors of Mu. They had access to advanced technology and science, but they needed funds to develop it. They assured me that once they had completed their work, the British Empire would benefit greatly from it. It seemed like a reasonable idea. A rather serendipitous coincidence, if you please. Discovering the possibility of genuine time travel and those who promised they could acquire it seemed to be perfect timing. We could benefit from working together, and no one else needed to know. I have enough influence in the government to request funds without question. It was all going very smoothly, until you stepped in. But from what you and your fishy lady friend are telling me, it is apparently a good thing you did. A point for you, brother."

Luna doused him again and replied, "Fishy lady friend indeed! Your reasoning smells worse than a two week old beached blue whale!"

Sherlock looked at Mycroft askance and flatly stated, "They never told you which empire would benefit from their actions, dear brother. You failed to see their true purpose. But they have been stopped. We have destroyed their bases, their ships, and their submersible factory. They are all in custody, even the ones that set off to free their associates near Iceland. They are all locked up, contained, and this is over. It is done. And so it seems even the great Mycroft Holmes is entitled to a human error now and then. But let there not be hard feelings between us. Let us share a cup of tea. You look as if you could use one."

While he was speaking, Luna had replaced the blanket over her tail, and Sherlock had poured two cups of hot water from the tea kettle in the corner of the office. He removed a small tin from his pocket and poured a greenish mixture into Mycroft's cup and handed it to his brother. "It was an interesting and worthy idea, Mycroft, but this time, you did not think it all the way though. You let the information get in the way of your judgment. I am sure you won't let it happen again."

He raised his cup and held it up for a moment, they saluted one another with their tea cups and drank their tea. "Do drink up, Mycroft. This tea will do wonders for you. It is seaweed based you know."

Mycroft finished his cup of seaweed tea, set it down, and immediately started blinking his eyes. He looked rather confused for a moment, turning his head first to the left and then to the right. Finally, he rubbed his eyes, opened them wide, and looked with surprise at his brother. "Sherlock, when did you arrive? I did not notice you entering. Why does your hair look darker? And what is that odd uniform you are wearing? Are you and Watson working undercover on a case? Your disguise would never fool anyone, you know. I knew it was you as soon as I noticed you were here. I must have been in a very deep concentration. I find it hard to believe I never saw you enter. When *did* you arrive? Do you, by any chance, know why I am completely soaked in salt water? And who is this lovely lady with you? A client?"

Turning to Luna, he addressed her, "Good day, madam, I hope you are well. Pardon my sogginess at the moment. I must have been out in the rain, or something. I assure you that whatever your problem is, you can count on my brother to assist you. And if I am not mistaken, this is the famous author, Jules Verne. What brings you to England and in the company of my renowned brother, no less? Has someone made off with the *Nautilus*? You will forgive my humor. I really am an admirer of your work. You have such a clear vision of technology. Submarines, airships, rockets to the moon. It is almost as if you have seen the future."

Luna translated Mycroft's comments, and Jules Verne smiled and answered, "Thank you sir, but I assure you, it is research, pure and simple research. Nothing more."

He then turned and winked at us.

Sherlock set his cup down and thanked Mycroft for his assistance. Mycroft stated he did not know what, if anything, he had done, and he was still wondering why he was soaking wet. Sherlock bid goodbye to his brother, and we left the office.

Chapter 23. A Most Unusual Conclusion,
(And a sad farewell, but an encouraging promise.)

With a sense of satisfaction at the conclusion of the day's events, we made our way back to the deserted pier, to once again, join the *Nautilus*. I did, however, make a quick detour to a ladies fashions shop and purchase a stylish hat for Luna to wear on our return journey back to the ship. I gave it to her and fondly said, "When we first met, you swam off with my hat. Here is one that will look much better on you, and you can keep it."

Luna giggled with delight and answered, "Why dearest John, that is so very sweet of you. You are right, though, this hat does look much better on me than it would on you."

We continued our way back to the pier in silence, each lost in our own thoughts on the extraordinary adventure we had just concluded. We were nearly there when Luna expressed that she was not feeling well. Her tail was very sore and hurting, unlike anything she had ever previously experienced.

Back inside the *Nautilus*, we discovered the material we had used to make her water skirt had caused a reaction with the scales of her tail, and that was the cause of the pain and discomfort. We moved our final gathering to the airlock chamber so Luna could be immersed directly in the sea water entry pool. She immediately felt much better. While the chair and water skirt had worked this time, it would not be healthy for her for any future usage. My heart sank when I heard the news.

We informed Captain Nemo of all that had occurred and assured him that the communication breech was closed, but he would have to continue using code instead of the Atlantean language for contacting his agent in the British government, since Mycroft Holmes still saw all communications of interesting or unusual nature.

Sherlock explained to us he knew had discovered the source of the leak, but was concerned until he had determined a way to properly address it. "I was actually testing the tea that time you looked in on me Watson, and I did not recognize you. I had to make sure I gave Mycroft the exact dose that would cause him to forget this whole episode, without affecting the rest of his prodigious memory and mental faculties. He is an extraordinary person, and important to the country."

"Yes," I replied, "and you bested him. And then you erased his memory of your doing so. That was kind of you, Sherlock."

"I did not do it out of kindness for him. I did it to protect the Atlanteans and Jules Verne, as well as Luna." Looking at Captain Nemo, he went on, "As you had mentioned when we first met, Captain, your group of Atlanteans must remain invisible to the rest of the world, so you may continue your task. And as H. G. Wells expressed in our previous adventure, the government cannot know of the existence of time travel. It is best kept a secret for now."

Jules Verne nodded with an all knowing smile, and said, "I agree completely. That is why, although I have quite often traveled in time, I have never written about time travel. I will never bring up the subject. I will leave it to H. G. Wells. I wonder though, where does he get his ideas? Invisibility serums and human animal hybrids? That is real fictional science."

Sherlock agreed and said, "Yes, but I think the term 'science fiction' sounds better."

As Sherlock and I prepared to leave the *Nautilus* and return to our flat, Captain Nemo stated that after we left, he would return Jules Verne to his former yacht, now under the command of Nemo's men, and that Verne would continue his short cruise on the yacht. No one would ever know what had happened. The world could not know what had happened. "You saved the world today, my friends. Thank you for your assistance in this effort. It could not have been done without you Mr. Holmes, Dr. Watson, nor without you, Luna." He turned to Sherlock and me, and continued, "I must apologize one more time for the tea ruse that I used to bring you aboard."

Sherlock grinned and said. "I understand completely, Captain Nemo. You needed to get us on board the *Nautilus*, so we could see for ourselves what you were saying was true. I bear no hard feelings."

I agreed and added, "But you must understand, that after this adventure, I will never touch another cup of seaweed tea as long as I live."

We laughed and Sherlock remarked, "I have enough information from this journey to write a new paper on *"The Multiple Applications, Usages, and Possibilities Derived From Seaweed Tea, With an Emphasis on Knockout Gas and Memory Inhibitors"*. And it has already been successfully field tested!"

Sherlock exited the airlock chamber, along with Jules Verne and Captain Nemo, to gather some items before we left. Luna had spent her time during the group discussion swimming in the salt water, and she was feeling back to her aquatic self. She gave a quick thrust of her tail and again was sitting next to me on the edge of the pool. Of course, I was once more drenched in sea water, but I did not mind in the least. I was happy to be near her one last time. It saddened me deeply to say good bye to her and know I would most likely never see her again. She looked at me and said, "My dearest sweet John Watson. You have been so kind and caring. You are beyond compare, and I give you this gift from my heart." She placed in my hand a golden seashell that had been strung on a strand of her long dark hair. On the shell she had written, 'Luna'. I thanked her profusely for it and removed from my pocket the poem I written for her earlier. I gave it to her, and she clutched it as if it were gold. With her lilting musical voice, she slowly read it aloud:

"The Mystic Magic Sea"

The sea is calling, hear its voice,
a mystic magic song.
Its spell, enchanting leaves no choice.
Its echo lingers long.

It weaves a web of salt sea air,
and tides that ebb and flow,
to lure you with a song so fair
that it seems to glow.

A sea of diamonds in the sun
glitters far and wide,
sparkling till the day is done,
drifting on the tide.

Now a mist is softly creeping
gently o'er the sea.
Soon the ocean will be sleeping,
quiet as can be.

The silver moon is now ascending
o'er the misty grey
bank of fog that's never ending,
drifting on its way.

Dolphins dance and mermaids hide
in the waters deep
where their secrets can abide
always for to keep.

The sea is calling, hear it sing,
a mystic magic tune,
that timeless will forever ring
beneath the silver moon. "

She held it close to her and exclaimed, "John this is truly beautiful! I will treasure and remember it always! I will remember you always. I promise you, John Watson, we will meet again. Someday…" Then Luna embraced me with a kiss that I shall never forget, dove back into the water, and she was gone.

I sat in silence for some time staring at the golden seashell in my hand and wondered if I ever would meet her again. I placed her precious gift in my pocket and left the airlock chamber to go find Sherlock.

We said goodbye to Jules Verne and Captain Nemo, stepped out on to the deserted dock, and watched as the *Nautilus* silently submerged beneath the waves and vanished into the endless mystery that is the sea.

Sherlock looked at me and commented, "Watson, you are soaking wet. You know, you are going to catch cold. You should take something for it. "

I turned to him and replied, "That may be, but don't you even think of suggesting seaweed tea."

He grinned and said, "No, I would not dream of it, but how about some nice hot seaweed soup?"

Post Script: Again?
(Yes, it can get even more strange and unusual.)

Three days later, I was still sick with a cold. Nevertheless, I had managed to record the two fascinating adventures we had so recently experienced, while the facts were still fresh in my mind. Sherlock and I were enjoying a cup of tea, and I can assure you it was most definitely not seaweed. I was eternally grateful to once again be savoring Earl Grey. We agreed that nothing could possibly compare to the recent episodes. We were certain we would never again experience anything so strange or unusual, when there was an odd clattering sound in the hallway outside of our door. It sounded almost like a horse's hooves, but more musical.

We were wondering what it might be, when the door burst open to reveal a knight in chain mail armor. He boldly stepped inside the room, and announced, "I am Sir Percival, knight of the Round Table of Camelot. In the name of King Arthur, High King of England, I seek to engage the services of one Sherlock Holmes in locating a missing person. That person being the Right Honorable, Alfred Lord Tennyson.

Also from Joseph W. Svec III

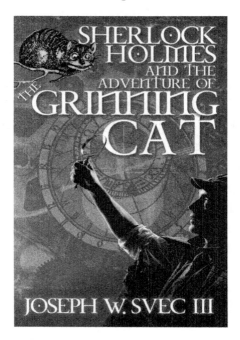

Sherlock Holmes and The Adventure of The Grinning Cat

"Joseph Svec, III is brilliant in entwining two endearing and enduring classics of literature, blending the factual with the fantastical; the playful with the pensive; and the mischievous with the mysterious. We shall, all of us young and old, benefit with a cup of tea, a tranquil afternoon, and a copy of Sherlock Holmes, The Adventure of the Grinning Cat."

Linda Hein, Hein & Co Used Books, and founding officer of the Amador County Holmes Hounds Sherlockian Society

Also from MX Publishing

MX Publishing is the world's largest specialist Sherlock Holmes publisher, with over a hundred titles and fifty authors creating the latest in Sherlock Holmes fiction and non-fiction.

From traditional short stories and novels to travel guides and quiz books, MX Publishing caters for all Holmes fans.

The collection includes leading titles such as Benedict Cumberbatch In Transition and The Norwood Author which won the 2011 Howlett Award (Sherlock Holmes Book of the Year).

MX Publishing also has one of the largest communities of Holmes fans on Facebook with regular contributions from dozens of authors.

www.mxpublishing.com

Also from MX Publishing

Our bestselling short story collections 'Lost Stories of Sherlock Holmes', 'The Outstanding Mysteries of Sherlock Holmes', 'Untold Adventures of Sherlock Holmes' (and the sequel 'Studies in Legacy') and 'Sherlock Holmes in Pursuit'.

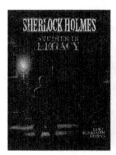